"I noticed you haven't been making my bed."

Hannah seemed mystified by Clayton's accusation. "Make the bed? Every morning?"

"Straighten the covers. Put the spread on top."

"But—you sleep in that bed."

"That's true. But only at night. It can sit here made up the whole day while I'm working."

"You should air it during the day so it'll be fresh at night. What benefit do you derive from it being made while you're gone? You'll only see it at night before you unmake it."

She stood beside his bed, inches away from him, looking at him tentatively. She was as wrong for him as any woman could be. But he wanted to pull her into his arms and sink into the unmade bed with her, and hold her all night and all day....

Dear Reader,

This April, let Silhouette Romance shower you with treats. We've got must-read miniseries, bestselling authors and tons of happy endings!

The nonstop excitement begins with Marie Ferrarella's contribution to BUNDLES OF JOY. A single dad finds himself falling for his live-in nanny—who's got a baby of her own. So when a cry interrupts a midnight kiss, the question sure to be asked is *Your Baby or Mine?*

TWINS ON THE DOORSTEP, a miniseries about babies who bring love to the most unsuspecting couples, begins with *The Sheriff's Son*. Beloved author Stella Bagwell weaves a magical tale of secrets and second chances.

Also set to march down the aisle this month is the second member of THE SINGLE DADDY CLUB. Donna Clayton, winner of the prestigious Holt Medallion, brings you the story of a desperate daddy and the pampered debutante who becomes a *Nanny in the Nick of Time*.

SURPRISE BRIDES, a series about unexpected weddings, continues with Laura Anthony's *Look-Alike Bride*. This classic amnesia plot line has a new twist: Everyone believes a plain Jane is really a Hollywood starlet—including the actress's ex-fiancé!

Rounding out the month is the heartwarming *A Wife for Doctor Sam* by Phyllis Halldorson, the story of a small town doctor who's vowed never to fall in love again. And Sally Carleen's *Porcupine Ranch*, about a housekeeper who knows nothing about keeping house, but knows exactly how to keep her sexy boss happy!

Enjoy!

Melissa Senate
Senior Editor
Silhouette Romance

Please address questions and book requests to:
Silhouette Reader Service
U.S.: 3010 Walden Ave., P.O. Box 1325, Buffalo, NY 14269
Canadian: P.O. Box 609, Fort Erie, Ont. L2A 5X3

PORCUPINE RANCH

Sally Carleen

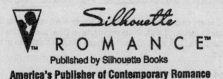

Silhouette
R O M A N C E™
Published by Silhouette Books
America's Publisher of Contemporary Romance

To Linda Steward and Sarah Reed
for letting me borrow their real ranch

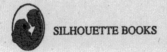

SILHOUETTE BOOKS

ISBN 0-373-19221-5

PORCUPINE RANCH

Books by Sally Carleen

Silhouette Romance

An Improbable Wife #1101
Cody's Christmas Wish #1124
My Favorite Husband #1183
Porcupine Ranch #1221

Silhouette Shadows

Shaded Leaves of Destiny #46

SALLY CARLEEN

For as long as she can remember, Sally planned to be a writer when she grew up. Finally, one day, after more years than she cares to admit, she realized she was as grown up as she was likely to become, and began to write romance novels. In the years prior to her epiphany, Sally supported her writing habit by working as a legal secretary, real-estate agent, legal assistant, leasing agent, an executive secretary, and in various other occupations.

She now writes full-time and looks upon her previous careers as research and/or torture. A native of McAlester, Oklahoma, and naturalized citizen of Dallas, Texas, Sally now lives in Lee's Summit, Missouri, with her husband, Max, their very large cat, Leo, and a very small dog, Cricket. Her interests, besides writing, are chocolate and Classic Coke.

Readers can write to Sally at P.O. Box 6614, Lee's Summit, MO 64086.

HANNAH'S HOUSEKEEPING HINTS

1)   **Housework is dangerous and should never be attempted by an amateur!**

2)   **Let sleeping dust lie.** Dust conforms to the laws of physics—it can change form, but will never disappear. So, don't disturb it when it's settled and not bothering anybody.

3)   **To clean the tub, toss some cleaner in the bottom.** The next person who showers can skootch around and clean the tub as they clean their feet. But if a cowboy slips and falls, don't run to his rescue. He won't be wearing any clothes—and he'll be very upset.

4)   **Allow unmade beds to air.** Never make up a bed that has just been slept in by a good-looking cowboy. This will provoke mental images of his unclad body, and every time you move the covers, you'll smell his scent of leather and earth.

5)   **Cooking is an imprecise science, more akin to alchemy.** Keep peanut butter, blackberry jam and a loaf of bread in the cupboard for times when experiments explode.

6)   **Don't ask for a diamond ring for your engagement—ask for a housekeeper!**

Chapter One

Hannah Lindsay rubbed her sweaty palms down the sides of her cotton skirt. Yesterday, she'd lost her mind or she never would have let Samuel talk her into coming out here. Today, she'd lost control of her body. No matter how hard she concentrated, she simply couldn't make her hand reach up and knock on the door in front of her.

She turned and looked wistfully back toward her small white car parked only a few yards away. The normally nondescript vehicle had been transformed into a bright, beckoning beacon against the dreary landscape. Tufts of grass, a few small cacti and several gnarled mesquite trees stabbed the flat, parched, brown earth, their green colors muted by the dust.

Only forty-five minutes south of San Antonio, Clayton Sinclair's ranch seemed light-years from her cozy condo in the heart of the city. If she drove really fast, she could make it home in forty minutes. Maybe thirty-five.

Behind her the door opened.

She spun around to see a huge cowboy standing in the doorway, glowering down at her.

Okay, maybe *huge* was an exaggeration, but he was definitely large, and he was definitely glowering.

She recognized Clayton Sinclair from the picture Samuel, his grandfather, had shown her. He was a younger, tougher, sun-bronzed version of his grandfather. Tall, like Samuel, but with much wider shoulders and a bigger chest, as if he wrestled two-ton steers before breakfast.

His hair was light, sun-streaked. Probably wrestled those steers after lunch in the midday sun, too. Squint lines fanned out from intensely blue eyes that seemed to burn from his deeply tanned face. Whoever said blue was a cool color? Hannah thought.

He wore faded blue jeans over a flat stomach and muscular thighs, and his faded denim shirt was open at the throat, allowing light brown curls to spring out. Clayton oozed virility and sexuality and he didn't look like *anybody's* grandson. This was going to be even worse than Hannah had anticipated.

"Can I help you?" he asked—demanded, actually—when she continued to gawk at him as if she were an idiot.

Things were getting worse by the minute. Talking to strangers wasn't easy for Hannah under the best of circumstances, and talking, under false pretenses, to a stranger who oozed sexuality didn't even rank in the top fifty percent of her list of possibilities. In fact, it was pretty darn close to the bottom. Right down there with the day she graduated from high school and was supposed to give the valedictorian speech…and froze in front of a thousand people.

She opened her mouth, but coherent words couldn't fight their way past the tense muscles in her throat. She gurgled.

That should make a terrific first impression. He'd probably send her packing before she figured out how to make her vocal chords work again.

So? Wasn't that what she wanted?

"Are *you* Hannah Lindsay?" he finally asked.

She had no idea what he'd expected, but she obviously wasn't it. The disappointed look on his face knifed straight into her heart. Suddenly she was back in her adolescent years when everything she did was a disappointment to her parents.

She nodded in answer to his question, giving up the effort to verbalize. The movement was a little jerky, but she was pretty sure it was the right one. Up and down with the head. Up and down. Good girl.

"You're applying for the job of live-in housekeeper?" He sounded resigned. If she hadn't known better, she'd have thought he knew all about her deficit in housekeeping skills.

She cleared her throat and straightened her spine. "Yes." That was much better. A squeak instead of a gurgle. A recognizable word. She was becoming practically verbose.

"I'm Clayton Sinclair. Come in." He stepped aside, holding the screen door for her.

She swallowed hard, took a deep breath and ordered her feet to take her into the big old ranch house. Right foot. Left foot. Breathe.

She almost lost cadence as she brushed past Clayton and the compelling scents of leather and open country overwhelmed her, painting a vivid mental picture of him on a horse, swinging a lariat and roping longhorn cattle. She'd better omit breathing from her walking sequence. One thing at a time.

With its high ceiling and drawn drapes, the large room was cool, shadowy, cavernous and ominous. She half expected a bat to fly out of a corner at any minute. Or out of her own personal belfry. Today's events certainly proved she had a few up there.

"Have a seat." Clayton indicated a looming, Victorian-style armchair patterned with large flowers on the back. Maybe the dim lighting was a good thing. She wasn't sure she wanted to see those flowers up close.

From long habit, she reached behind her to shove things aside before she sat down, but the chair was empty. No books, papers, computer disks, shoes. That was probably one of the things housekeepers did. Kept the chairs empty. She had no empty chairs at home, not even after her housekeeper came.

She perched on the edge. Ready to run...to escape.

Clayton sat on a long red sofa a few feet away. It was empty, too. Until he sat down, anyway. He filled up a good portion of it and looked totally out of place on the formal, feminine furniture.

"The position involves a lot of work," he said, crossing one booted foot over the other knee with relaxed, unconscious masculinity.

The gesture added one more layer of tension to the mass already squirming in Hannah's stomach. Nothing could make this ordeal easy, but it would have helped if Clayton had been short and pudgy.

She didn't try to talk this time. Best to save her effort for when he asked her a direct question.

"Keeping this place clean isn't an easy job," he continued. "As you can see, my mother furnished it pretty elaborately. It's not my style, but she comes back to visit every month or two, so I like to keep all her tables and vases and—'' He waved a negligent hand around the room, and Hannah noticed lamps, statues, bowls...even a bird cage decorated with flowers. A lot of wasted space, it seemed to her. Nothing that served any practical purpose.

Her survey of the room ended with the painting over the fireplace. Samuel would be pleased to know it was still there. He was right. His wife had been a beautiful woman, but even in the portrait she looked frail.

''The floors are all hardwood and have to be polished, except the kitchen,'' Clayton went on. ''It's linoleum and has to be waxed. Then there's the laundry. I have five ranch hands who'll be here through the spring roundup. They stay in the bunkhouse, so you don't have to clean for them, but you will be expected to do their laundry as well as mine, and you'll cook for all of us, three meals a day.''

He paused, peering at her intently. Unfortunately, her eyes had adjusted to the dimness, and she could see his dubious expression quite clearly. He didn't for one minute think she could do all those things.

Well, she couldn't, so why did his attitude upset her? She could design complex computer programs as easily as most people wrote letters, but her cooking skills stopped with peanut butter and blackberry jam sandwiches or an occasional frozen dinner.

She ought to stand up, agree with Clayton, thank him for the interview and leave. She'd promised only to come out here and *apply* for the job. She could honestly tell Samuel she'd done her best. And she had warned him there was no way she'd actually be hired.

Stand! she ordered her legs. *Up!*

They ignored her.

She wasn't surprised.

"Your former employer gave you a glowing recommendation," Clayton continued.

"Glowing recommendation?" she repeated, her surprise conquering her nerves sufficiently to give her a voice.

Omni Software, Inc. had given her a glowing recommendation as a housekeeper?

That was impossible. Of course they hadn't. He must be trying to let her know that he knew who she was and knew this whole thing was a hoax.

She dropped her head, letting her masses of unruly hair fall protectively forward. She should have felt relief that it was all over, but instead her cheeks flooded with embarrassment.

It wasn't enough that she looked like a complete idiot in front of Clayton Sinclair, now she'd been exposed as a deceitful idiot.

"Yes, your employer said you were the best housekeeper he's ever had." Clayton's tone was dry and unenthusiastic...a little angry, she thought. Not that she blamed him, considering the circumstances. "Actually I didn't talk to Mr. Taylor directly."

Hannah gasped, her head snapping upright at the mention of the surname Samuel had taken years ago when he'd awakened in a mental hospital in California, unable to remember his last name or how he got there. By the time he'd fully regained his memory, he'd already begun his business under that name and had kept it.

What had Samuel done?

Clayton frowned at her gasp, then continued.

"Glen Ramsey, my banker, tells me that Mr. Taylor, who's one of his major depositors, has given you a good reference and would really appreciate it if I'd hire you. This message comes from my banker who holds the note on this ranch—a man I really need to keep happy."

Now she knew what Samuel had done. Pressured somebody at the bank to pressure Clayton. No wonder he'd been so unconcerned about her lack of skills! The game had been rigged from the beginning.

If she got out of there without having a stroke, she'd kill Samuel.

"I'm sorry he did that," she mumbled, staring at the floor, again letting her hair fall forward around her face, embarrassed at her friend's tactics.

She rose on shaky legs. Less shaky than when she'd come in, though. Now she had a purpose. Make it home to kill Samuel.

Clayton heaved a long sigh. "No, no. Sit back down. It's all right. I don't have applicants for this job lined up for ten miles down the road, and even if I did, I wouldn't have time to interview them. I need a housekeeper, and I need one now."

Hannah lifted her head. Surely he wasn't saying what it sounded like he was saying.

He ran a hand through his hair, shifting the strands of light and shadow. She could almost feel the coarse texture, the warmth brought inside from days of working in the sunshine.

And sweating under a cowboy hat, she told herself in an unsuccessful effort to shut down her flight into fantasy. This was a real, working cowboy, not someone from a movie.

Somehow that thought made Clayton even more attractive.

"I don't like being pressured, but, on the other hand, I really don't care how I get a housekeeper as long as I get somebody who can do the job. Samuel Taylor assured my banker that you're a very competent housekeeper and that you could handle the work with no problem." A slight frown darted across his features, creasing his forehead between his eyebrows and making his jawline look even more square. "I just didn't expect you to be so..." He spread his hands, moved them close together then far apart.

Hannah watched in tense fascination, wondering what he hadn't expected her to be.

"My former housekeeper was fifty years old," he said, "and, uh, sturdy. Mrs. Grogan could throw a hundred-pound sack of feed over her shoulder and carry it to the barn. Not that you'd be required to do that, of course."

Hannah straightened her admittedly slim shoulders. Was he suggesting she couldn't heft a hundred pound bag over her shoulder and carry it to the barn?

"You think I can't?"

He looked at her dubiously, and her shoulders slumped.

Certainly she couldn't. Why did it bother her that he had pointed out the obvious? She couldn't cook or do laundry or polish floors, either, so why should she feel indignant and upset that he wasn't going to hire her to do just that? Hadn't she learned after all these years that it was pointless to try to succeed at activities for which she had no ability?

"We've been three weeks without a housekeeper," he went on, ignoring her dumb question. "Mrs. Grogan left unexpectedly when her mother up in Oklahoma had a stroke. Last week she called to say she was going to have to stay there. My extra hands for the spring roundup came on two days ago, and the five of them have been complaining ever since about having to eat sandwiches after doing the work of ten men.''

He slapped one big hand on his denim-covered thigh, making her jump. "Okay, so you're young and, uh, slim. I guess neither one of those problems is fatal. We're in a financial crunch right now and I probably can't start you at what you were making, but if the salary I mentioned in the ad is okay, you've got the job."

Hannah fell back into the chair.

"The job?" she croaked. "I've got...?"

Chapter Two

Clayton studied his new housekeeper curiously. Her disjointed response to his job offer was the oddest he'd ever encountered. While he resented his banker's pressure tactics, at the same time, he'd been relieved that his search was over. He was ready to hire the woman and be done with it.

His comment that he didn't have time to interview a lot of applicants had been a gross understatement. This was the busiest time of the year as well as the most expensive, what with the extra hands. Every minute he spent interviewing cost him money—and money was something that was in short supply, especially with the continuing drought.

He hadn't had any doubts about hiring Hannah Lindsay until he'd opened the door and seen her standing there, looking terrified and completely out of place.

She was a little taller than average, but so slim he was afraid the first strong west wind would blow her away. Big brown eyes peeked out from masses of shiny, dark brown, curly hair that almost hid the rest of her face. How was she going to keep that hair out of her eyes when she leaned over to scrub floors? Her clothes weren't very housekeeperish, either—a blouse with long, puffy sleeves, a vest and a long flowing skirt. She looked like some kind of an artist, much too unworldly and fragile to handle the ranch.

She'd come into the stuffy old house trailing the scent of roses, and she had a look about her that made him think of a spiderweb with a drop of dew on it, quivering in the morning sunlight. He wanted to touch her, feel the translucent skin of her delicate face.

Clayton clenched his callused hands and mentally ordered them to keep away from that porcelain skin. He'd threaten the other guys within an inch of their lives if they got out of line with her, too. From the looks of her, he didn't think she'd be able to deal with the rough characters he'd hired for spring roundup.

Nevertheless, this Mr. Taylor had given her a great reference, and, even if he had a choice after Glen Ramsey's *persuasive* phone call, he was desperate.

"My banker said Mr. Taylor has already closed up his place and left for Europe, and you'll be able to move in and start work immediately." Those big eyes got bigger. Did she not understand what he meant? "Can you start work soon? Tomorrow? Today?"

"Tomorrow?"

He wasn't sure if she was repeating something she didn't comprehend or agreeing to start tomorrow. He elected to put the positive slant on it. "Then I'll see you in the morning."

"Morning?"

She really did have some major communication problems. Thankfully, cooking, washing and cleaning didn't require a lot of communication. "As soon as you get up, you get dressed and then come on out here."

He stood.

She stood.

"Would you like to see your room?"

She shook her head, the motion jerky but a definite negative.

"In the morning, then. I'm very pleased to have met you, Ms. Lindsay." He offered his hand to shake and after a second's hesitation, she took it.

Her hand was slim, smooth and soft in his. Again the word *fragile* came to mind. And tantalizing as that concept might be to Clayton's male ego, it wasn't a good one for a housekeeper on a ranch in Texas brush country. Out here, only the strongest survived.

Reluctantly Clayton turned her hand loose even as he fought an urge to pat it and smile and reassure her...and *not* hire her to take care of his house.

He moved to the door and opened it.

She came to life then and, with a wild-eyed look, darted out the door, across the yard, into her car and peeled away in a cloud of dust.

Clayton shook his head as he watched her go. Such a pretty girl. Too bad she was so odd. Maybe her mother didn't take enough vitamins when she was pregnant.

He made a quick check to see if they had enough lunch meat and bread for dinner. Damn! They were running low on mayo. Thank goodness he could stop worrying about things like that come tomorrow.

So what if Hannah Lindsay was a little strange, a bit off center? She had great references.

From an elderly man who lived in a condo, not a crew of half-civilized cowboys on a completely uncivilized ranch.

Determinedly ignoring the nagging voice of doom, Clayton went out to continue vaccinating the hundred plus head of cattle they'd rounded up that morning. The men would work even harder knowing they'd soon have decent meals.

Hannah went straight to Samuel's apartment, ignoring her own door across the hallway. She banged on the door with one fist while she repeatedly jabbed the doorbell with the other.

The older man opened the door almost immediately. "Did you meet him?" he asked before she had a chance to say anything. Just seeing him standing there looking so hopeful took the heat from her self-righteous anger.

His physical resemblance to her own grandfather was superficial, but the kindness in his blue eyes, his uncritical acceptance of her, his caring attitude were hauntingly reminiscent of the man who had been her world. She wanted to return his caring, to do everything she could for him, all the things she hadn't been able to do for her grandfather because he'd died too soon.

"Come in and tell me about my grandson," he said. "How did he look? What did he say?"

"How could you do this to me?" She tried to force indignation into her tone. "You called somebody at the bank and lied to him, and now I've got the job as your grandson's housekeeper!"

"But Hannah, you agreed to do it for me."

Hannah spread her hands in frustration. "I agreed to apply for the job, but I never dreamed I'd get it! I told you I wasn't going to lie about my qualifications."

"And that's very admirable of you, but not very practical. That's why I had to lie *for* you. If you didn't get the job, how could you get to know my grandson? How could you smooth the way for me to meet him in person and not just in this cold, flat picture my detective took of him?"

Samuel looked so sad, so lonely. In the six months since he'd moved in across the hall from her, he'd become a dear friend, and she knew how much this meant to him. She wanted to help him.

But she couldn't.

She'd already crumpled under the impact of Clayton Sinclair's disapproval. She'd had more than enough disapproval in her life. Working as Clayton's housekeeper guaranteed she'd give him plenty of occasions for more.

"Samuel, you know how hard it is for me to talk to people I don't know."

"You didn't know me when I moved in here."

"But you were so friendly, and you reminded me so much of Granddad. It wasn't like you were a real stranger."

"You'll get to know my grandson even faster since you'll be living there."

Hannah shook her head remembering the way Clayton looked in his blue jeans and western-cut shirt, the way he'd crossed one booted foot over his knee, the easy air of strength and masculinity. She'd love to get to know him...in another lifetime, of course, when she'd be a confident, sexy woman whom he could be interested in.

But she couldn't tell Samuel that.

"You know I don't even like to go to the grocery store. I'm only comfortable when I'm home with my computer, designing my games."

"I know that. I also know the company in Dallas wants you to make personal appearances in an advertising campaign to demonstrate the latest game you're working on and you told them no. That proves it's time you get out into the world, get away from the computer and experience life. Going to Clayton's ranch and doing this for me will be a great place to start."

Hannah shook her head. She'd thought Samuel understood that she was experiencing the only life she wanted to experience.

Opting to change her approach, she turned, walked over to her own door and flung it open. "Look in here and be logical. How can you possibly expect me to clean house and cook for anybody?"

Samuel came to stand beside her and survey the controlled chaos that was her home—stacks of papers, drawings for graphics pinned to chair backs and thumbtacked to walls, books sprawled here and there with protruding bits of paper marking pertinent pages, articles of clothing sprinkled throughout and other odds and ends.

"Look," she repeated, waving her hand through the air. "Not one empty chair. Clean houses have empty chairs. I haven't seen my carpet in so long, I don't remember what color it is. I live on peanut butter sandwiches, chips and dips, frozen dinners and colas because I don't know how to cook."

Samuel wrapped an arm about her shoulders. "There you go again, underestimating yourself. You can do anything you want to do. How many times have you told me that everything anybody needs to know can be found in books? I just happen to have a book on cleaning house as well as a cookbook."

Good grief! He had this all planned out! Just like the call to the bank!

"Even if I could do it, I already have a job! I'm under contract for *Unicorn in the Garden*. They're willing to live without me being a part of the advertising, but they do want the game finished in time to feature it in their fall catalog of computer games. I have a deadline!"

Samuel took her arm. "Please, Hannah. I'm counting on you. Let's go over to my place where I've got empty chairs. I'll fix you a nice cold cola, and we can talk about this."

"No." This *no* wasn't quite as firm, she noticed with dismay. Surely she wasn't going to let herself be talked into this insanity.

"It'll only be for one day, maybe two."

"Oh, right. Like he's not going to notice by the end of the first day that I haven't done any cooking or cleaning." But she found herself allowing Samuel to lead her into his apartment. Saying *no* to him was so difficult, just as she'd never been able to say *no* to her own grandfather.

Beyond that, she realized with a sinking feeling, some perverse part of her actually wanted to go back to Clayton's ranch and prove to him that she could do everything Mrs. Grogan had done. To see approval in those piercing eyes.

Jeez! She really had lost her mind.

* * *

Shortly after ten-thirty the next day, Hannah's teeth rattled as she drove over the cattle guard onto Clayton's ranch.

In the back seat she had two of the outrageously expensive suitcases her mother had given her for high school graduation, the large one full of clothes and the small one containing Samuel's cookbook and housekeeping manual.

No doubt about it. She'd slipped a gear, gone mental—she was, in the vernacular, *nuts*.

Especially considering she was halfway—well, maybe a quarter way—excited about this venture, about seeing Clayton Sinclair in his faded denims and scuffed cowboy boots again, even if she could only grunt or gurgle at him.

A giant ERROR message flashed across her mind at that thought. She'd feel Clayton out about his grandfather, tell him how sick with grief Samuel had been, convince him Samuel would never have deserted Clayton's mother if he'd known he had a grandson on the way, and then she'd get out of there quick. Before night.

She focused on the road stretching ahead, a dry, colorless ribbon leading to the house. A glance in the rearview mirror showed nothing but a giant cloud of dust roiling in her wake, following her. As omens went, it didn't seem like a very good one.

Clayton swore under his breath as he tried to herd a group of ten normal cattle plus one rambunctious young bull who seemed to think this was all a game.

Usually he kind of agreed with the bull.

Cattle could be difficult creatures, and trying to

raise them in the tough brush country only made it worse. Nevertheless, he loved everything about the life, every ornery cow, every dry bit of sand, every prickly cactus, every twisted mesquite tree.

His mother, born and raised in the hill country of Austin, had hated their home as passionately as he loved it. As a child, Clayton had resented her attitude, had almost taken it as a personal rejection. But he'd come to realize that the land was simply too harsh for her. She'd have escaped years ago if she hadn't been left alone and pregnant, the despised ranch, belonging to her dead husband and missing father-in-law, her only home and means of support.

Gradually Clayton had taken over the management, but it was only when he reached the age of twenty-one that she'd turned over the books to him. He'd discovered then how badly she'd mismanaged the ranch, even taking out a mortgage on the place.

He'd never blamed her. She'd done the best she could. She'd just been unsuited for the ranch.

He took a great deal of pride in the fact that he was pulling it out of debt in spite of everything.

The long drought was taking a heavy toll. With most of his herd under optimum weight, he desperately needed rain. But even without it, he'd manage. This was tough country, a worthy opponent, and that was what he loved about it.

Normally, working the cattle, mending the fences—any of the necessary tasks—brought him contentment and took his mind off all the problems. But today had gotten off to a lousy start and hadn't improved a bit so far.

He'd wasted most of the morning hanging around

the house waiting for Hannah Lindsay, his taste buds anticipating his first hot meal in three weeks.

Not to mention that he wouldn't mind seeing a pretty female face after looking at nothing here lately but unshaven, ugly cowboys and hairy, smelly cattle. Even if she couldn't talk, Hannah was real easy on the eyes.

She was also a no-show. Hadn't even phoned to say she wasn't coming. She'd probably realized she wouldn't be able to hack it out here and had run for her life.

He forced himself to pay attention to the task at hand and finally got the young bull headed in the right direction.

He'd take this group to the corral, then go back to the house and make ham sandwiches again. It was ten-thirty already, and last night he'd promised the over-worked men that they'd have real food for lunch. Now he would have to disappoint them.

As he neared the corral, he saw a cloud of dust rolling toward his house. That was strange. The only visitor he expected today had been Hannah Lindsay.

Irritation and disappointment washed over him anew at the memory of her failure to show up. He'd been right about her. She was too much like his mother, her soft fragility unsuited to the land's harshness.

From the corner of his eye, he noticed that the rebellious bull, apparently taking advantage of Clayton's momentary distraction, had separated from the group again.

Cursing Hannah Lindsay and whoever was stirring up that cloud of dust, he went after the bull.

When he finally got his cattle settled in the corral,

Clayton headed toward the house. As he approached, he recognized Hannah's little white car.

His first impulse was delight. She'd come after all.

Several hours late, he reminded himself, his guard automatically going up. Being late for the first day wasn't a good sign. Out here they didn't have the luxury of being late, especially in the mornings.

He tried to push his doubts aside. Maybe she'd had car trouble. Maybe she'd gotten lost. Considering the peculiar way she'd acted yesterday, that was certainly a possibility.

The important thing was, Hannah was here. He had a cook and housekeeper. That was the only reason he was so glad to see her.

Then he saw her slim figure heading across the yard, back toward her car. Was she leaving? No, he couldn't let her do that! He urged his horse to a full gallop.

She stopped with the car door open and looked toward him, apparently hearing the sound of his horse's hooves. Her dark, luminous eyes were visible even from a distance.

He reined up beside her and dismounted, amazed at how excited he was to see her in spite of his earlier misgivings. But he supposed that was understandable. He was as tired of eating sandwiches as the men were. Not to mention that he was running out of clean underwear.

"Hi," he greeted her, smiling as he pulled off his hat and wiped the perspiration from his brow in one practiced movement. "When you didn't show up this morning, I was afraid you'd decided not to take the job."

She looked puzzled, pushed the car door closed

then checked a large, black-banded watch that was much too big for her thin wrist. At least it was practical; not one of those thin gold things. He told himself that was a good sign.

And with that observation, he realized that he was looking for good signs. He was desperate for good signs, and Hannah didn't carry many with her.

She lifted her deer-caught-in-a-headlight gaze from the watch to him. "It is," she said. "Morning."

Clayton bit the inside of his lower lip and clenched his hands. This was not a good sign.

"I don't know what kind of a schedule your former employer had, but around here, morning comes quite a bit earlier, like about 5:00 a.m." He spoke as softly and calmly as possible. He didn't want to scare her off.

Nevertheless, she flinched as though he'd slapped her.

"Five? Is the sun up then?"

Oh, brother. They were in trouble. And yet he felt like a jerk just for telling her the hours she was expected to work.

That was a dumb thing to feel. If she couldn't handle it, she had no business being here.

Taking a deep breath, he slid his hat back onto his head, momentarily blocking his view of her. It was easier to scold her when he couldn't see that vulnerable look on her face.

"No," he said. "The sun isn't up at that hour. We have to get an early start. I should have told you yesterday. Never mind. You're here now. Think you can put together a quick lunch?"

"Lunch?"

Well, he wasn't hiring her to make speeches.

Surely her cooking skills were better than her verbal ones.

"Where are your bags?"

Reluctantly, it seemed, she looked toward the car. "In there." Her voice sounded as if her throat needed to be oiled.

He took the key from her, opened the car door and hauled out two designer suitcases. He wasn't paying her what she'd earned before if she could afford bags like those.

But by the end of the season, he should have the mortgage paid off. Then next year he'd turn a profit, and he'd make it up to her.

As though she was likely to be around next year. Mrs. Grogan had lasted for three years. Except for his mother who hadn't had anywhere else to go until she met her new husband, that was pretty much a record. His father and grandparents were gone before he even arrived on the scene. Most people didn't fare well out here. Nothing was permanent except the land and him.

But he could hope Hannah would last a year or two. Hiring and training new employees took time away from work.

"Come on. I'll show you where everything is in the kitchen. Mrs. Grogan always stayed pretty well stocked up, but if you need anything, you can order it this afternoon and it'll be delivered in the morning. I know that's harder than going to the store and getting things yourself, but we're so busy this time of the year, nobody leaves the ranch unless it's an emergency."

"Nobody leaves?" Hannah repeated, somehow

managing to fill each word to bursting point with panic.

What on earth was the matter with her? Clayton wondered. She sounded as though she'd been sentenced to life in a maximum security prison. She'd just taken the job. Surely she wasn't already planning to leave. That would set a new record, even for this ranch.

Chapter Three

Nobody leaves the ranch unless it's an emergency?

Clayton's words hit Hannah smack in the gut like a bad case of botulism.

So much for her plans to be out of there before night. Clayton wasn't talking about just a day or two. Did this *emergency* thing mean she'd have to burn down the house to get out? Or would a complete nervous breakdown be sufficient?

Hoping for a sudden time warp to fold around her and drag her anywhere but where she was, Hannah followed Clayton's towering figure across the yard and into the house.

His broad back and denim-clad thighs made her blood run hot on the way to her heart and cold on the way back as she thought of having to face him, talk to him. Or maybe it was all running at the same time, sharing the same vein. The way she felt right now, anything was possible. Except, apparently, that time warp. She remained stuck in the here and now.

Clayton led her upstairs to a large, dark room at the end of the hall. Large dark furniture, including a four-poster bed, loomed at her. She was supposed to sleep in this mausoleum?

He deposited her bags inside the door. "Your bathroom is two doors down. Sorry it's not private. This house was built before we had indoor plumbing this far out of the city."

Not private? Hannah gulped at the thought of sharing a bathroom...and sharing it with this overwhelming male person.

"Of course, the only visitors we ever have are my mother and her husband. So, except for the fact that you have to go out in the hall, it's pretty much private." Hannah released a soft sigh of relief mingled with a tiny hint of disappointment that Clayton apparently had his own bathroom. "Clothes closet through there, linen closet in the hall," he continued, obviously unaware of her personal drama.

Clayton checked his watch, and her gaze followed his, noting the sunbleached hairs curling from his shirt sleeve, surrounding the leather band.

"Ready to fix a little lunch for six hungry cowboys?" he asked.

She nodded, wondering if a lie had to be verbalized or if movement counted. Lying by omission, lying by nod.

She was ready for a lot of things—to run screaming from the house, to murder Samuel, to press the hairs on Clayton's wrist and watch them spring back, but she was in no way ready to *fix a little lunch.*

Wondering how the heck she was going to get out of this one, Hannah went downstairs with him to the big kitchen. As he pointed out the location of all the unassembled food components, she made an effort to memorize everything he said.

Flour in the big canister, sugar next, then coffee. Cans of food in the pantry.

The peanut butter jar greeted her like an old friend in a world of strangers. She wanted to embrace it. She didn't see any blackberry jam, but there was a big jar of strawberry preserves. That would do. She *could* make lunch after all.

"Through that door is the laundry room and a big freezer with plenty of meat and vegetables."

She could check that for the possibility of frozen dinners.

"I know it's late," Clayton said, standing behind her, his warm breath stirring her hair. "You don't need to come up with anything elaborate. We've been eating sandwiches so long, anything else will be welcome."

Anything else? So much for her lunch plans. Back to square one.

For a long moment he didn't move, just stood there behind her so close she could smell his leather, sunshine and warm earth scent that teased her senses and somehow made her feel even more confused.

He needed to leave so she could catch her breath. So she could go upstairs and look up *lunch* in the cookbook. Surely he didn't plan to wait around for her to make the meal? How in the world was she supposed to look it up then figure out how to do it with him watching?

"So," he said, "what do you need to get started?"

She turned to look at him. He *was* planning to wait around and watch her.

In desperation she pointed upward. "I need—"

"Oh, sure," he said, stepping back. "You do remember where the bathroom is?"

The bathroom? Oh, well. It didn't matter what he thought she was doing as long as she could get to that cookbook. Hannah nodded, then darted away and charged upstairs.

She opened the small bag and hurriedly flipped the cookbook open to the index, to the *L's.*

*Liver...*surely they wouldn't expect her to make that.

*Lobster...*oh, she loved lobster thermidor. When she'd lived at home, she'd frequently asked their cook to make it. This wasn't going to be so tough after all.

Lunch dishes. There it was! She turned excitedly to the page.

Soup and sandwich. No, that wouldn't do. Clayton had nixed the sandwiches.

Pasta salad. Perfect! She loved the colorful curly pasta and all the little bits of goodies.

If she could program a computer, surely she could do this. Other people cooked all the time.

She winced at that thought, her parents' oft-repeated statements playing again in her head about what *other* people could do. *All your friends have learned to dance. All your friends can make small talk with the guests at parties and dinners. All your friends make their parents proud of them.*

Being able to understand advanced calculus and quantum physics or program a computer hadn't helped her then.

But now she had specific directions, and she could follow directions, she told herself reassuringly.

The recipe purported to be adequate for four people, so she'd better double it to feed seven. She read it twice, carefully doubling and memorizing every measurement, every detail.

Clayton smiled eagerly at her when she came back down to the kitchen. He had a nice smile. His white teeth made his tan look even more golden and turned the crinkles around his eyes into sunbursts. For a brief, unreal instant, she fantasized that the sparkle in those eyes was for her, but she knew it was only because he was hungry, and he expected her to feed him. Her own lips turned upward at that ridiculous thought.

His expression seemed to soften as if a haze settled around his face. "Nice." He spoke the single word quietly, almost indistinctly. It sounded like *nice*, but that made no sense. It was completely out of context.

"Ice?" she questioned. That would be logical since they were dealing with food.

"Huh?"

"Rice?" she guessed desperately. "Mice?" Surely not.

He shook his head and cleared his throat. "What do you need first?"

"Pasta," she said, hoping he'd forget about the rice...or those mice. "A sixteen-ounce package of pasta." Maybe he'd leave once he was sure she knew where things were located.

"Pasta?" He opened the pantry door, reached behind some boxes and came out with a huge package of spaghetti. "Like this?"

She shook her head. "No. Curly, colored pasta." She moved to check in the pantry herself, but he moved at the same time...directly into contact with her. Her hands went up in automatic defense and encountered soft, warm denim with the feel of solid muscle beneath—Clayton's chest. As if that wasn't bad enough, she felt his hands on her shoulders, steadying himself.

The hot blood rushed to her face, to her hands where they touched him, to her shoulders where he touched her. Every one of those spots felt much warmer than 98.6 degrees. Was this how cases of spontaneous combustion occurred?

"Sorry," he mumbled, backing away, taking his odd heat-producing properties with him. "I'd, uh, better go check on the guys. Tell them lunch is on the way. In, what, half an hour? Forty-five minutes?"

"Forty-five minutes. Sure." She had no idea if that would be long enough, but she'd have agreed to anything to get him to leave.

His going made the kitchen seem much larger and more open. She could breathe deeply now. She'd surely be able to get through this cooking ordeal a lot more easily.

So why did the large, open kitchen feel so empty?

Shrugging off the inexplicable feeling, she started scrounging through the pantry, looking for pasta. She couldn't find any of the colorful, curly kind, but she did unearth a couple of packages of macaroni. A monochrome start, but the bits of olives and other components should liven it up.

Following the advice of the recipe, she checked the package directions for the pasta and carefully measured enough water for both packages into a pan, then set it on the stove to boil.

This was easy. Why had she worried? She was going to be able to do this.

In her mind's eye she could see Clayton sitting at the head of the big oak dining table they'd passed on their way to the kitchen. She could see a big smile spreading across his face, tilting the corners of his eyes, as he tasted his first bite of her pasta salad.

Stop that! she ordered herself. What was the matter with her? She was no longer an insecure teenager, falling all over herself in a vain attempt to please everybody she met. She had only to please herself. Clayton's opinion wasn't important.

She focused on the macaroni package directions. *Cook six to nine minutes or until tender.*

Six to nine minutes or until tender? What the heck kind of direction was that? A thirty-three and one-third percent variance with an open-ended conclusion? She could just see herself writing instructions for her computer games like that. *Click left mouse button six to nine times or until something you like happens.*

This cooking certainly was an inexact science. In fact, anything that nebulous could hardly be called *science* at all. It was more like alchemy.

But somehow she had to figure out these ambiguous instructions.

After all, if she didn't prove herself competent, why would he listen to anything she had to say about his grandfather? That was absolutely the only reason she wanted to impress him.

Clayton washed up at the outside faucet down by the barn with the rest of the men.

"Okay, fellas," he said, trying to locate a semi-clean spot on the community towel to dry his own hands, "the new cook got here a little late, so lunch won't be anything spectacular, but at least it won't be sandwiches."

Mugger and Dub threw their hats into the air, Bear punched Cruiser on the shoulder, Bob slapped his knee and yelled "Hot Damn!" and everyone cheered.

"And one more thing." They quieted immediately, and Clayton realized he'd used his *this-is-important-so-you'd-damn-well-better-listen-close* voice. Well, it was important. "Hannah—Ms. Lindsay—is a little different from Mrs. Grogan. She's, uh, quieter, younger, prettier—"

Cheers broke out again, interspersed with whistles.

"The first one of you gets out of line with her, I'll break your face." The words came out loud and harsh.

Silence ensued as the men looked at each other.

"No problem, man," Bob mumbled.

"You got it, boss," Mugger agreed.

He hadn't intended to snap at them even before they'd done anything. On the other hand, better before than after. Hannah's big brown eyes were bottomless pools of innocence. If one of the men did anything to destroy that innocence, he'd do worse than break the guy's face.

"Ms. Lindsay is, um, different," he said.

"You already told us that," Bear growled.

"I said she was different from Mrs. Grogan. Now I'm saying she's different from everybody."

"You mean she's not right in the head?"

Clayton flinched at the brutal description. Hannah wasn't crazy. At least, he didn't think so.

"She's different," he concluded obscurely. "Let's go get some lunch."

"All right!"

The men followed him up to the house and into the dining room where the table was set with his mother's dishes with their elaborate floral design. His fault. He should have told her to use the plain brown ones he'd bought after his mother moved out. Well, it wouldn't hurt the men to eat off pink and purple flowers. They probably wouldn't even notice in their excitement over their first hot meal in two days.

"Where's the food?" Bear demanded.

"Sit down. She'll be out in a minute," Clayton said confidently. But he didn't feel all that confident. No tempting odors drifted from the kitchen the way they did when Mrs. Grogan cooked.

Hannah appeared in the kitchen door carrying a serving bowl with a spoon sprouting from it. Her hair looked even wilder than usual, and her eyes had a glassy look. She hesitated, her gaze taking in the ruffians who were talking and laughing as they settled into the chairs at the table. Her entrance froze them in place, Cruiser and Dub already poised over their chairs.

"Ms. Hannah Lindsay, this skinny guy here is Dub. The big, fierce one, with so much grizzled hair and beard all you can see is the tip of his nose, is Bear. The one with the trim little gambler's mustache is Mugger. The long drink of water is Cruiser, and the redhead's Bob."

Hannah's gaze went from one person to the next, all around the table, her expression getting wilder with each cowboy. When she came to Clayton, a bright red spot appeared on each smooth cheek. "Lunch," she blurted, holding the bowl before her.

Cruiser ran to take it. "Let me help you, ma'am."

Hannah's face relaxed enough to allow a tentative smile as she surrendered the bowl. Yes, she definitely had a nice smile. "Thank you," she said in a relatively normal voice.

Dub stumbled from his half-sitting position and pulled out her chair at the end of the table nearest the kitchen.

"Thank you," she said again, looking and sounding a little more confident. She was communicating coherently, and the blood was redistributing itself from her cheeks to the rest of her body. That was an improvement.

Cruiser scooped out a large spoonful of food from the bowl and plopped it onto his plate. Macaroni mixed with bits of black, green and red sprawled among the painted flowers. Nobody said a word as all attention turned to the concoction.

"What is it?" Cruiser finally asked.

"Pasta salad." Her voice was again strained as she dipped her head, letting her hair fall over her face.

"Pasta salad," Clayton repeated before any of the men could say something to upset her more. "Great. This should give us a chance to cool down. Pass that bowl over here."

Knowing the others would be watching him and following his example, he scooped out a generous serving. "Looks terrific."

He took a bite of the stuff. The pasta was way past *al dente*. In fact, it was more like *al mushe*.

He looked down to the other end of the table. Hannah was watching him expectantly, her heart in her eyes.

"Good," he said, thankful he'd had a new lightning rod installed last year. That kind of a lie could bring down divine retribution. "Needs a little salt. Maybe a little picante sauce." Texas picante sauce could cover a multitude of bad flavors, or in this case, no flavor.

The men poured on the picante sauce and ate without grumbling, but he was sure he'd hear about it later.

They'd just have to cut her a little slack. She hadn't had a lot of time to cook today, and maybe her last employer liked overcooked pasta salad for lunch. She'd never worked on a ranch before. He'd have to explain to her that they preferred heartier meals.

She's not going to make it, a little voice nagged in the back of his mind. *You knew that from the minute she walked in here. Roses bloom in town, along the river. Prickly pear cactus is the only flower that thrives out here.*

He knew that little voice was probably right, but he ordered it to shut up anyway.

"All right, boys. Back to work." He folded his napkin and laid it on the table. "I'll be down to the corral in a few minutes." He slid back his chair.

Hannah watched the other cowboys push away from the table. They'd been every bit as gracious as any of her mother's guests, but she knew they were disappointed.

She grabbed an armload of dishes and ran into the kitchen, away from the censure that was in the air if not actually spoken.

She'd blown it again.

She'd wanted to run out of the room the minute Clayton had looked up with a pained expression and declared her meal to be "good." But she'd had to sit at the table while everyone poured on enough picante sauce to drown any noodles that had survived her excessive boiling, then choked down the horrible mess.

She couldn't go through that much stress again. She had to work up the courage to talk to Clayton about his grandfather then escape before dinner.

How did some people manage to cook three of those things a day?

Clayton came through the kitchen door carrying the empty serving bowl.

"Have you got a minute?" he asked, setting the dish on the counter. "We need to talk about something."

Hannah couldn't remember any good conversations that began with that statement. Here it came. He was going to fire her. She wouldn't be able to help Samuel.

But what really clenched her stomach into hard little knots was knowing Clayton viewed her as a failure.

Damn it, why did she care what he thought of her?

She braced herself, straightening her back and looking him in the eye. "Yes?"

Clayton stood for a moment gazing at her, his eyelids drifting to half-closed. He lifted one hand and pushed her hair back from the side of her face, his fingers barely stroking her cheek.

Her breath caught in her throat. The touch set off little sparks, and she wanted him to continue doing it.

When his hand fell away, her belligerent hair sprang right back as if his fingers had never been there. But the skin he'd stroked remembered. Something inside her remembered exactly the way his touch had felt.

"You smell like roses," he said softly, his lips forming the words as though caressing them, and she wondered how those lips would feel if they replaced his fingers on her skin.

"My grandfather loved roses," she whispered, trying to force her thoughts away from such fanciful thoughts. "He—"

She couldn't remember what she'd been about to say. The expression on Clayton's face took her words away. Took her breath away for that matter. He looked like one of those men in the movies just before they kissed the girl.

She was fantasizing again! Why would Clayton want to kiss her?

But what if he did and found out that she could no more kiss than she could sing, dance, play piano or make small talk at parties? She'd die of embarrassment if that happened!

"What?" she croaked.

He blinked. "Huh? What?"

"You wanted to talk to me."

"Oh. Yeah. I did." He drew a hand over his own cheek and chin—the same hand he'd touched her hair and cheek with. "I wanted to talk to you about…oh, yeah. About lunch. I know this is a big change for you from your last job." That was the quintessential understatement! "But there's a little difference between cooking for a retired man and cooking for a bunch of cowboys. We do a lot of physical labor, and we like our meals to be hearty. Roasts, chicken, meatloafs, bacon and eggs for breakfast, things like that. Protein. Food for energy."

Of course he hadn't been thinking about kissing her. He'd only been thinking about criticizing her.

Clayton sounded just like Hannah's dance teacher after she'd broken her toe in class, like her voice teacher when he told her he'd had to buy ear plugs and hide the crystal, like her parents who'd finally given up on her and let her go her own way.

Well, she thought, thrusting her jaw forward and clenching her fists, she'd left all that behind her. She wasn't going to give in to it again. Her own way hadn't been so bad.

"We usually eat around seven. Can you get something together by then?" he asked.

"Of course I can," she blurted, surprising herself with her bravado. "And I won't break my toe doing it, either!"

Chapter Four

Clayton got out of the house as fast as he could, climbed onto his horse and rode toward the corral at a gallop.

He'd almost kissed Hannah Lindsay. What the hell had he been thinking?

He hadn't been thinking. That was the whole problem. Something about Hannah Lindsay scattered his brains the way the west wind scattered the dust.

He'd better maintain a little more control in the future. That was the last thing he needed right now— to get involved with a delicate, sweet-smelling flower, inhale her scent, touch her butterfly soft lips—

His self-reprimand wasn't going too good. He'd better rephrase it.

He didn't need to get involved with a woman who'd turn his brain to mush, distract him from the ranch that required all his attention, especially now. A woman who, like his mother, would soon wilt in the scorching Texas sun.

If he'd needed proof of her fragility, he'd gotten it when he'd criticized her luncheon fiasco. She'd lifted her head bravely which only added to her look of vulnerability, emphasizing the hurt in her dark eyes.

But even as he'd seen that hurt and felt guilty for causing it, he'd also seen her lips, slightly parted, full and tempting. He'd had to fight the urge to pull her into his arms, comfort her, kiss away the pain, replace it with desire. Her hair had been soft when he'd touched it, and she'd made a barely audible sound that was somewhere between a gasp and a moan.

Every emotion showed on Hannah's open face. As clearly as he'd seen the pain, he saw that she'd wanted him to kiss her. And, heaven help him, he would have if she hadn't been the one to interrupt.

He had an uneasy feeling that Hannah Lindsay was going to cause him some real problems. Or maybe that uneasiness just came from the pasta salad with picante sauce that was crouching in his stomach like a spicy, soggy rock.

He reined in at the corral.

Dub looked up, pulled his hat brim low over his face and tugged on the reins to turn his horse to ride away.

"Didn't hire that one for her cooking, did you?" Bear guffawed as he plunged a vaccination needle into a big Simmental's rump.

Clayton scowled. "One more comment like that, and you're all out of here." In shock and disbelief he listened to the words coming from his own mouth. Had he really said that? What would he do if even one of the men walked? Every able-bodied man in the area was already working on one of the various ranches.

Dub halted and thumbed his hat back from his face. "I been seeing signs of a porcupine around here," he drawled. "Looks like he's been trying to eat these tough old mesquites and live oaks. After he's been on an awful diet like that, I'd sure hate to run into the prickly critter."

Clayton shifted in his saddle, aware of the implied comparison. "Sorry, fellas. I didn't mean to snap."

Hannah was causing problems, and she wasn't even around.

Except in his thoughts.

Mugger rode up. "We got a break in one of the irrigation lines down in the hay field."

"Damn! Okay, let's go take a look." Clayton turned his horse in that direction, surprisingly relieved at having a crisis to handle. Even though they couldn't spare the precious water draining away, a broken irrigation line would be a simple, straightforward problem compared to Hannah.

She had to make dinner. Hannah didn't see any way around it. She found some chicken breasts in the freezer and a recipe for chicken Kiev in her cookbook. It was a short recipe, and a dish she'd always enjoyed eating. Surely Clayton and the other cowboys would like it.

With the chicken thawing, she looked around in bewilderment. What was she supposed to do now? Without her computer, she felt lost.

She tried to recall what her housekeeper did. Sweep, mop, dust, vacuum. But the details were sketchy. While Mrs. Henson cleaned, Hannah worked, completely involved in her computer, with the rest of the world tuned out.

She wandered into the living room and drew a finger across the smooth surface of one of the multitude of small tables. Even in the dim light, she could see the mark. However, she'd always felt that being able to write your name in the dust didn't count—it was only when the sides of the letters collapsed.

Nevertheless, she could probably dust. She went upstairs to the linen closet and got a washcloth. That should work.

As she was starting back, she noticed the dark outline of a computer screen through the half-open door down the hall. She hesitated, then decided that was as good a place as any to start dusting.

The minute she walked in, she felt right at home. No empty chairs here. Papers, manuals, account ledgers and dozens of unopened bank statements were strewn everywhere, including on top of a massive old wooden desk that took up one side of the room.

Over the desk hung a portrait of a young Samuel. This must be the companion to Martha's picture downstairs.

So Clayton did care about his grandfather after all. She studied the photograph for a moment, but her gaze was inexorably drawn to the computer sitting quietly in the midst of the chaos on the desk. It looked to be strictly an out-of-the-box deal. Packing cartons were shoved into the other corner. But at least it was a computer, a new, state-of-the-art computer, and she was drawn to it like an addict.

She swiped a hand across the computer screen. It was really dusty! How could Clayton let his equipment go like that? She yanked open the desk drawers but couldn't find compressed air anywhere.

Using the washcloth, she cleaned as best she could

then turned it on just to be sure the dust hadn't damaged the hard drive. Everything seemed to be in working order.

Checking the directory, she found the basic programs that would have come already installed as well as an accounting program she'd co-authored while she was still with Omni Soft.

If Clayton used her software—though, of course, he'd have no way of knowing she'd helped design it since the copyright was with Omni Soft—it was indirect acceptance of something she'd done.

Oddly pleased, she shoved invoices and bank statements off the desk chair, then sat down and opened the file.

Garbage!

Somebody had started to input data and got it in all the wrong places, resulting in confusion of the categories and generally making a mess.

Fortunately, she could straighten it out.

Sometime later she sat back with a satisfied sigh. Her poor program had been abused, but she had things all set up now and had even changed a few options to personalize it to the ranch. Clayton could complain all he wanted about her cooking skills, but whoever did his computer work should be shot.

Omigosh!

Cooking!

That silly recipe for chicken Kiev said it had to sit in the refrigerator for an hour, and a quick glance at her watch told her she'd never have time for that.

She turned off the computer and raced downstairs to the kitchen. At least the blasted chicken was thawed. Now it had to be pounded to an eighth of an inch.

Locating a ruler was no simple matter. She found an old one in the back of one of the drawers of the desk in the office. After her catastrophe with cooking the macaroni too long, she took extra care about measuring the chicken.

One-eighth of an inch exactly.

If you didn't count the holes.

She found some toothpicks to hold the meat around the butter until it was chilled. Since she didn't have an hour, a few minutes in the freezer would have to do.

Scalloped potatoes would have been nice to serve with her chicken Kiev, but she didn't have time to deal with another complicated recipe. Baked should work.

She checked the book. An hour and a half at 350 degrees. Since she only had an hour, she'd have to increase the temperature by one-third, which came to 466 degrees. But the oven thermostat was broken into increments of 25 degrees. She chose a setting between 450 and 475, closer to 475.

On her way back from returning the ruler to the office, she paused to look more closely at Martha's picture.

Samuel must have loved his wife very much. Thirty years she'd been dead and he'd never remarried. Just the way Hannah's own grandfather had been about his beloved Phoebe. She'd died when Hannah was a baby, and Granddad had never looked at another woman.

Of course, the first two years after Martha's death, Samuel had been in severe depression, unable to cope with losing his only son and his wife, unable even to remember who he was. But after he'd begun to recover, found himself in California and started Taylor Industries, a successful manufacturing firm, he'd probably had plenty of opportunities to remarry.

How wonderful it must be to have somebody love you so much.

The painter had captured an inner glow on Martha's face. She looked happy and content in spite of too-prominent cheekbones and soft shadows under her eyes. The portrait had been done only a year before her death. Mentally Hannah moved the picture of Samuel from Clayton's office to hang beside her. She could see him reaching out of the frame, taking Martha's hand, gazing down at her, his glow matching hers.

She could almost see them moving around this house, not always together but never apart, the way people comfortably in love would do. The blinds would be open, the place light and full of love and happiness....

Clayton pulled off his boots, muddy from repairing the broken irrigation line, then stepped onto the porch. As he approached the door, he saw Hannah standing in the living room, gazing up at the portrait of his grandmother.

He should take her to task for wasting time when so much work needed to be done, but even through the screen, he could see the wistfulness to her stance and the tilt of her head.

He opened the door quietly, as though he feared disturbing whatever spell she was under...or casting. He crossed the room, his sock feet making no noise on the thick rug. As he came up behind her, the faint scent of roses wrapped around and drew him closer to her.

"She was my grandmother," he said, his words coming out hushed, almost reverent, unconsciously and unavoidably matching the atmosphere she created.

"I know," she answered dreamily.

Well, there you go. So what if she couldn't cook, Clayton thought. The woman was psychic. From her tone she almost sounded as if she were in a trance.

"She's beautiful," Hannah continued, her breath whisper soft, and he remembered his first impression of her as a spiderweb quivering with one glistening drop of dew.

"She died before I was born," he said. "But everybody says she was a wonderful woman."

"I'm sorry. That she died, I mean. Of course I'm not sorry she was a wonderful woman."

Hannah could talk after all. And in her offbeat way, she even made a bizarre kind of sense.

"Samuel should be up there with her," she said.

"Samuel?" This was getting eerie. How did she know his grandfather's name?

"He loved her so much."

"I guess he did. Too much."

His words came out unintentionally harsh and barren. She whirled around, her dark curls leaping about her face, her eyes wide and startled as if she'd just that moment realized he was there.

"Oh!"

So much for her garrulous phase. Back to words of one syllable.

But she swallowed hard then shook her head. "No.

You can't love somebody too much." She eked the words out almost painfully.

Clayton folded his arms and studied her. He didn't like talking about his grandfather, especially not to strangers, but he didn't want to discourage Hannah's attempt at conversation. He didn't want to see the distress of rejection on that guileless face.

"My grandfather didn't have any inner strength. Without her, he collapsed. He built this place from the ground up. You'd think that would mean something to him. But after my dad was killed and my grandmother died, he just disappeared. Never came back. Never even called to see how things were going."

"But it must have been very hard on him, losing his only son and his wife."

"Of course it was hard when he'd let them become his only reason for living. He was selfish and irresponsible."

She shook her head. "You don't know that. You don't know what happened to him or how he felt."

Clayton's mother had complained a thousand times about her father-in-law's selfishness in leaving her alone and pregnant on a ranch she hated. Even as a child, Clayton had tried to comfort her and repeatedly assured her he'd never desert her. For as long as he could remember, his grandfather had been a reverse role model for him. Everything the older man had been and done, he'd avoided. He'd never hated his grandfather the way his mother did, but he had always resented him.

Now with one comment, Hannah was making him wonder what had happened to the man, if everything really had been so simple.

"It doesn't matter. He's probably dead by now. What I do know is, when the chips were down, he wasn't strong enough to hack it." And he didn't want to discuss it any more. "What are we having for dinner?"

"Oh!" she said again. "Chicken. It's time to fry the chicken."

"Fried chicken? Hey, that sounds great!"

She smiled up at him, her eyes dancing. "You'll like it."

With that she darted away.

Fried chicken for dinner. That was encouraging, better than pasta salad.

He looked up at his grandmother's picture again. He hadn't realized Hannah had such a romantic bent. He hoped she wouldn't bring up the subject of his grandfather again. The past was gone; there was no changing it and no point in dwelling on it. Stirring up old anger didn't accomplish anything.

Odd that she'd known his grandfather's name. Clayton was sure he'd never mentioned it to her. Maybe she really was a little psychic. As strange as Hannah was, as strange as she made him feel, almost anything was possible.

He started up the stairs to wash for dinner, then stopped halfway. *Samuel.* That was her former employer's first name. *Samuel Taylor.* So maybe she wasn't psychic. Maybe she was just a little nutso, confusing her former employer with his grandfather.

The whole thing was very strange.

He diverted his mind to the fried chicken. *That* was totally mundane and solid.

Hannah closed the kitchen door behind her and tried to stop shaking. She'd become so involved in

fantasizing about Samuel and Martha's life that she'd
forgotten where she was, forgotten to be careful. For
a few other-worldly moments there she'd imagined
some kind of ethereal bond with Clayton. Then she'd
admitted to Clayton that she knew the woman was his
grandmother and, to top it off, had mentioned his
grandfather's name!

She had taken the opportunity to try to talk to Clayton about his grandfather, but hadn't made much
progress.

Samuel was right about one thing. Clayton wasn't
going to welcome him with open arms. He probably
wasn't going to be too happy with the messenger,
namely her, either.

For several long minutes she waited for Clayton to
come after her, to accuse her of deceiving him, to
throw her bodily off the ranch. If he did that, she'd
curl up in a little ball and shrink to nothing from
humiliation at being caught, but at least she wouldn't
have to do any more cooking.

When he failed to show, she made a quick reas-
sessment and, reluctantly, made the decision to finish
dinner.

Her calculations must have been off, because the
chicken was frozen, and the toothpicks refused to
come out. She studied the fused elements. She really
didn't have much choice except to fry it "as is."
Nobody would have to ask for a toothpick later.

While the chicken Kiev was cooking, she took the
potatoes from the oven. One side had gotten a little
dark and hard, but they were big potatoes. There
should be plenty of the soft, white part left.

She set one on each plate on the dining room table

and put out the butter. She felt good about the potatoes.

She went back and lifted the chicken from the grease. It didn't look like any chicken Kiev she'd ever had. She didn't feel as good about it as she did about the potatoes.

From the dining room just outside the kitchen door, she could hear the men arriving, laughing and talking. She even heard Clayton's voice promising them fried chicken.

Maybe if she stayed in the kitchen long enough, they'd eat their baked potatoes and go to bed.

Maybe she could run out the back door, get in her little car and drive away. Keep driving and never see Clayton or Samuel again.

Maybe her fairy godmother would come along and transform this mess into something edible.

Since none of those things was likely to happen, Hannah took a deep breath, picked up the platter of chicken Kiev, or whatever it had metamorphosed into and went through the doorway.

Calls of "Food's here!" and "Yeah for the cook!" dwindled to silence.

At the end of the table, Clayton looked surprised, then shocked, then he covered his face with his hands. That wasn't good.

"Fried porcupines?" Bear asked uncertainly.

Chapter Five

Hannah froze. She couldn't move, couldn't even turn around and run back into the kitchen to hide from this latest failure. She was doomed to spend the rest of her life standing at the foot of the table, paralyzed with humiliation, clutching a platter of fried porcupines.

"Well, bust my britches," Dub exclaimed, rising from his chair and coming toward her. "Just like my mama used to make. Here, let me help you with that, little lady. Can't hardly wait to wrap my mouth around one of those critters." He took the platter from her nerveless fingers.

"It's—" The word came out a squeak. She cleared her throat. She couldn't have them thinking her catastrophe was some sort of exotic dish. Did they really fry porcupines? "It's chicken."

"Yes, ma'am." Dub sat down and helped himself to a particularly bristly specimen.

"One of my favorites," Bob drawled, taking the platter from Dub.

Hannah sank slowly into her chair. The men were being kind...kind above and beyond the call of duty. There was no way they could really mean what they were saying. "It isn't supposed to look like that."

Mugger sawed off a bite, popped it into his mouth and chewed. "Mmm mmm," he enthused. "Who cares what it looks like 'long as it tastes good?"

"It does? Watch out for the toothpicks," she warned.

"Heck, little fiber never hurt a body," Cruiser said, taking a porcupine for himself and passing the platter on to Clayton.

Hannah held her breath to see what Clayton would do. He took one of the creatures, eyeing it dubiously as if he half expected it to attack him.

"Whaddaya know," Bear said from the other side of the table. "Crunchy baked potato. I always enjoy my food more when it talks back to me."

As if sensing her gaze on him, Clayton looked up and gave her a forced smile. He wasn't buying all the false praise from the men anymore than she was, though she felt a warm spot for the effort they were making. That effort, rather than any faint belief in their words, made her feel a little better, though not better enough to offset Clayton's obvious disappointment.

Her heart went soggy and heavy, kind of like the noodles they'd had for lunch. This situation wasn't working. If Clayton didn't fire her before the meal was over, she would leave as soon as she cleaned up the mess in the kitchen. The men would be a lot better off eating sandwiches, and she'd definitely be a lot better off at home working on her computer. Creating programs was one heck of a lot easier than creating food.

A sharp stab of guilt knifed through her at that resolution. She'd failed at helping Samuel. His grandson had no desire to see him, and she hadn't done one thing to change that.

All well and good to console herself that she could be successful with computer programs, but when it came to people, she was still a miserable failure.

Clayton took his time getting dressed after his shower. He knew he was stalling, putting off what had to be done. There was no room in his operation for Hannah Lindsay. He had to fire her. Competence was the bottom line, and Hannah wasn't even in the space between the lines on that one.

He'd never before had the slightest qualm about slicing the deadwood from his operation. Business was a cut-and-dried affair with no room for emotions. So why did he dread telling Hannah?

It was *not* because he didn't want her to leave. Of course he wanted her gone. She was a terrible cook. So what if she had an ethereal, helpless appeal that made him want to pick her up and carry her across the burning, sticker-infested sands—barefoot.

That was exactly why she had to go. She was even less suited to this place than his mother had been. She'd never survive out here, and he didn't have time to baby-sit her.

Go down and do it, he ordered himself. She wasn't any happier with the situation than he was. He could tell that from the scared, desperate way she'd looked at dinner. He'd be doing her a favor. She'd be relieved to get away.

Determinedly, he strode from his bedroom and down the stairs.

Hannah entered the living room from the opposite side, coming from the kitchen. She looked up at him, her eyes deep ingenuous pools, a startled expression on her open face, and Clayton felt his resolve melting away.

"Well." He smiled a too big, forced smile. "Got everything cleaned up?" What was the matter with him? Why was he making idle chitchat? Why couldn't he just get on with it?

"Yes," she said. "It's...all clean."

He cringed at the way she hesitated before saying it was all clean. If she cleaned as badly as she cooked, what did the room look like now? Would it ever be usable again?

"Did you have any problems?" he asked.

"Of course not." She sounded a little defensive. "I had a minimum amount of trouble figuring out the dishwasher, but I managed."

She had trouble figuring out the dishwasher?

Okay, so maybe he should give her the benefit of the doubt. Maybe there was a lot of variation in dishwashers.

"Have a seat." He waved a hand vaguely around the room. "You must be tired." It couldn't be easy making such a phenomenal catastrophe of dinner, then having to clean up the mess, and Hannah didn't look as if she were used to coping with hard work.

She moved over to a chair, looked back at it as if she expected to find something lurking there, then settled on the edge—the same way she'd done yesterday when she came in for an interview—the frightened, vulnerable way that squeezed his heart.

He took a seat on the sofa and reminded himself that he couldn't afford to feel sorry for her. She wasn't doing her job, and that was all there was to it.

Feeling sorry for her? Are you sure that's what you're feeling?

There was that irritating, disagreeable voice in his head again.

"Dinner was terrible," she said, her eyes wide with sadness, her full lips quivering slightly.

"I've eaten worse." Clayton almost turned around to see who was standing behind him, who had made that ridiculous statement. He couldn't believe the words had come out of his mouth. But they had.

One dark eyebrow arched upward quizzically, and she studied him in silence for so long he thought they must be back to nonverbal communication. "What?" she finally asked. "What did you eat that was worse?"

"Uh, well..." Clayton pushed his fingers through his hair, buying time, trying to remember the worst meal he'd ever had. Probably lunch, but he didn't think that answer would do much toward removing Hannah's anxiety.

She twisted her pale, slim hands in her lap, knotting the fabric of her long skirt, and Clayton fought an impulse to go to her, take her hands in his and soothe away her tension.

Soothe her? He had to fire her. That's what he had to do. Those two actions were *not* compatible. They could *not* be done simultaneously.

"I can't do it," she announced with unaccustomed firmness. "I can't cook and clean for you."

Thank goodness. This was going to be easy. All he had to do was agree with her.

"Of course you can." Omigod! That ventriloquist was putting words in his mouth again.

She tilted her head sideways, her eyes round with astonishment. She wasn't any more astonished than he was. But at least that look of desperate sadness and fear had vanished from her delicate features.

"Everybody gets nervous when they start a new job," he added. If he kept *firing* her at this rate, pretty soon he'd be giving her a raise.

"Yes, but...you don't understand," she blurted. "I can't do it."

Oh, he understood that all too well! "Your former boss thought you could do it. Mr. Taylor gave you a great reference."

She stared down at her hands, her hair falling forward over her face. "I'm afraid he wasn't completely honest with you."

So her boss had lied about her qualifications. That explained a lot. But she must have done something right when she worked for him or he wouldn't have wanted her to find another job so badly that he'd lie for her.

Unless the man just wanted her out of his house. Unless he was somewhere in a hospital suffering from malnutrition or food poisoning.

"Were you fired from your last job?"

She looked up indignantly. "No! Certainly not."

"Then what's the problem? Why did you say you can't do the job?"

Her gaze drifted to a spot above his head. He wasn't sure if she was avoiding his eyes or watching invisible spiders cavort. "This is quite different from my last job. It's different from anything I've ever done before.''

Clayton considered that. It verified what he'd already known. Being on a ranch was a lot different from being in town, even for something as basic as cooking and cleaning.

"I'm a failure," she said. It was the second statement she'd made with certainty, though it was only a continuation of the first—*that she couldn't do the job.*

"Don't say that," he objected. "You can do anything you want to do." His words disproved his own point. He was doing a lousy job of firing her even though he was positive he wanted to.

"No, I can't. I never learned how to dance or sing or talk to people or—"

"Dance or sing?" He stood abruptly and extended a hand to her. "I don't know about singing, but I can teach you to two-step in two minutes."

That's good, that annoying little voice inside his head whispered sarcastically. *Somehow you've gone from firing her to teaching her to dance. Next you'll be offering her tenure.*

She shrank away from him. "My parents sent me to dance class, and the teacher sent me home. This isn't something I do well."

"What kind of classes? I'll bet they didn't include the Texas two-step or the Cotton-eyed Joe."

She shook her head again, but allowed him to take her hand. She looked exquisitely guileless and fragile, like one of those porcelain dolls his mother collected.

As he pulled her into his arms, he knew with a leaden burst of clarity why he'd lost his mind and decided to teach her to dance. His libido had taken control of his subconscious and invented this giant excuse just so he could hold her. Maybe she couldn't cook or dance or talk, but just the thought of her sure could do things to his body.

As Hannah moved into Clayton's arms, she was certain she'd taken leave of her senses. Last week she'd been a card-carrying Mensa member. But from the moment Clayton opened his door and entered her life, she became a blithering idiot.

First she let him find out the hard way that she couldn't cook. Now she'd somehow gotten herself into the position of letting this good-looking cowboy try to teach her to dance—something she was even worse at than cooking.

If she had any active brain cells left, she'd pull away and leave now, preserve whatever infinitesimal part of her dignity remained. But Clayton's touch had changed the firing patterns of her neurons. Instead of pulling away, she found herself pressing closer against him. His body was hard and solid, and he smelled clean, like soap and new leather.

"Okay," he said, his voice oddly husky. "Just relax. This is an easy dance. Follow my lead."

Oh, yes. She'd almost forgotten. They were supposed to be dancing, a feat that had, under the best of circumstances, always been impossible for her. Now she was supposed to accomplish it when her head was spinning, her legs had turned to overcooked noodles, and she couldn't even feel the floor beneath her feet.

"One big step backward with your left, no, your right, no...uh, with this foot." He nudged her right thigh with his. Sparks from the point of impact shot through her, reaching every cell.

She moved back woodenly, staggering only a little. Not too bad, all things considered.

"Good." He sounded as breathless as she felt. "Now back with the other foot." Again his thigh touched and seemed to melt into hers. She focused on making the requested movement, concentrating harder than she'd ever concentrated on quantum physics.

"That's good," he whispered. His arm wrapped around her waist pressed her closer as if he sensed she was about to fall. It wouldn't be the first time. She'd fallen before while trying to dance, and that had been without the added unbalancing factor of Clayton's body sending hers into a frenzy.

It seemed as if they hadn't moved for some time. She wasn't sure if this was part of the dance or if her perception of time and movement had become distorted.

A low, involuntary moan started in Hannah's breast and issued...from Clayton's mouth.

No wonder she hadn't been able to control the sound. She'd felt it moving up Clayton's chest and thought it belonged to her, thought it was an echo of the painful ecstasy Clayton roused in her. All the time it had been him.

Did that mean he was feeling the same things she was?

Even as the possibility occurred to her, she realized the evidence had been growing, as it were, since they'd begun their dance. Through his blue jeans, she could feel his hardness against her stomach.

She leaned back, looking up at him in amazement. He gazed down at her from half-closed, smoky eyes.

Hannah froze. Her heart was beating at Pentium

speed, but she couldn't seem to get her breath. Was he going to kiss her? What if she couldn't do this right, either? Where was her nose supposed to go?

His lips touched hers, and her brain ceased to function, turning over complete control of her body to her hormones.

Amazingly, her lips knew exactly what to do. Somehow, with no instructions from her, they responded to Clayton's.

His kiss was warm and soft and sent currents tingling through sections of her body far away from her mouth. It filled her with heady, intoxicating sensations as if she were performing a flawless ballet on a cloud. She moved closer to him, needing all of her to touch all of him, to explore and revel in every aspect of this incredible experience.

Even the floor beneath her feet felt different...soft and lumpy.

She was standing on his feet.

Chapter Six

Hannah jerked backward, smack against an external barrier. She whirled around, grabbing at the small, three-legged table, catching it before it hit the floor but not before a dark blue crystal vase slid off and shattered into a thousand colored pieces.

Hannah righted the table and knelt in front of the ruined vase, her latest catastrophe. Only she could break something in the middle of the world's greatest kiss.

"I'm so sorry! It was beautiful!" One of the few beautiful things in the house.

Clayton knelt beside her. "It's all right. It wasn't your fault."

She focused determinedly on the broken glass, unable to force herself to meet Clayton's gaze, to see the disappointment she knew would be there.

"Oh, look! There was something inside." She lifted the piece of yellowed paper from the blue confetti and unfolded it. Samuel's unmistakable hand-writing scrawled across the sheet.

For my marvellous, matchless, "munderful" Mar-tha— The vase is the color of your eyes. The roses are the color of my love for you. Always, Samuel.

Hannah's own eyes misted at the expression of Samuel's lost love. The man she'd grown close to because of their mutual aloneness had written this note in a former lifetime. With a heart full of happiness, he'd put pen to paper, then given the note to Martha. Hannah could imagine the happy glow on Martha's face as she read the words.

Clayton leaned closer to examine the note, then sat back and shrugged. "My grandfather wrote it to my grandmother. Notes like that were everywhere when I was a kid. Mom threw them away every time she found one. She must not have known he gave this vase to grandmother or she'd have trashed it."

"Trashed it?" Hannah exclaimed. "Why would she have trashed something so beautiful, some-thing…something with so much love behind it?"

Clayton studied her silently for a moment. "What is it about my grandparents that gives you the power of speech?" he finally asked.

"Well, I…" Hannah stood, brushing imaginary dust from her skirt. "It's just that…I don't understand why you don't love your grandfather." She pushed the words out quickly before they had a chance to dig in their heels and balk. She had to do this for Samuel. Her own grandfather had died before she'd graduated from college, before she'd had time to justify his faith in her, to prove herself worthy of his love. Now she had the chance to prove herself to Samuel, to help him.

"I loved my grandfather so much. He was my whole life. You mentioned my rose perfume." She ignored the blush she knew was flooding her face as she recalled the circumstances of his making that comment. "Granddad's roses always grew bigger and better and had more fragrance than anybody else's. When I smell roses, I think of him, and it makes me feel secure and loved and...and more confident." *A little more.*

Clayton stood, extended a hand and lifted her up beside him. For a brief instant she thought he looked wistful. Then he dropped her hand and motioned her toward the big chair.

She took a seat, careful not to lean back against the unnatural flower garden, and folded her hands to stop their trembling. He sat down across from her on the red sofa and studied her intently. Her folded hands began to tremble in unison.

"You're an unusual person, Hannah Lindsay," he said softly. That was, she thought, a kind way to put it. Better than calling her squirrely or flaky or a walking disaster.

"You're—" He hesitated and searched her face as if expecting to find an explanation of her written across her forehead or down her cheeks. She could have told him it was useless. As many times as she'd looked in the mirror, she'd never found anything to explain her *unusualness.* "At first I thought you were, uh, well, simple. Simple to figure out, I mean. But that's not it. You just keep yourself hidden way down deep inside."

Hannah felt herself blushing even more fiercely at Clayton's words. He had no idea how true they were, how much she was hiding! Somehow she didn't think he'd be any more impressed with her hidden depths than with her cooking or dancing.

"My grandfather always told me I shouldn't try to be anybody but me," she said, the words coming out almost defiantly.

"He was a wise man," Clayton said. "We run into all kinds of trouble when we try to be something we're not."

The truth of that homily had certainly been proven by her recent experiences.

"I was lucky to have him." Maybe if she told Clayton about her grandfather, he would see how meaningful and important such a relationship could be and why he should forgive Samuel for being less than perfect. "Granddad was always there for me. He believed I could do anything I wanted to do. He encouraged me to—" She probably shouldn't say that he'd encouraged her to study computer science. He might wonder why she was masquerading as a housekeeper. The two areas certainly weren't related. "He encouraged me to pursue my dreams. To do whatever I wanted, no matter what my parents or anybody else thought."

Clayton's lips quirked upward in a wry smile. "I can relate to wanting something different than your parents wanted for you. For as long as I can remember, all I wanted was this ranch. My mom wanted me to go to school and become a lawyer or a doctor or anything that got me away from here. It was very frustrating to have to wait until I was old enough to do as I pleased."

Hannah nodded. "I tried very hard to do what my parents wanted, but I couldn't."

"What was it you couldn't do?"

"Everything that mattered to them. They both grew up poor, and they worked hard to make money and be *socially acceptable,* something I couldn't ever seem to be."

"What is this *socially acceptable* garbage? You don't run down the streets naked or use bad language. What's the problem?"

Hannah found herself smiling at Clayton's appraisal of her social skills. "I have a hard time meeting new people. I can't go to a party and make small talk with strangers. I always stand in a corner somewhere and wish I could disappear through the floor. If Granddad was there, he'd tell me stories about all the people. I don't know if he made them up or if they were true, but they were wonderful stories and made it a little easier for me to talk to them."

Clayton shrugged. "A lot of people are shy. You're talking to me now."

Hannah blushed at the awareness that she was, indeed, talking to him as though she'd known him all her life. She looked down at her hands and realized that, amazingly, they'd stopped trembling. Maybe after being so intimate with him, dancing and kissing, she felt more comfortable.

Wrong! The trembling started again at the memory.

"That wasn't the only thing I couldn't do right," she blurted, yanking her thoughts away from that direction. An admission of her failings would be much easier and less embarrassing than to think about that dance and that kiss. "I took tap dancing and fell into the audience, and Granddad tried to pretend it was all part of the act." To Clayton's credit, he didn't laugh, though she suspected from his facial contortions that he wanted to. "I took ballet and broke my toe, and

Granddad lied and told me Baryshnikov broke his whole foot when he was young. No matter what happened, Granddad was there to make it bearable."

"He sounds like a terrific person. You're right. You were lucky to have him in your life."

"I don't know where I'd be today if not for him." She took a deep breath and prepared to turn the conversation. "Grandparents are great. They love you without all the expectations you get from parents. Wouldn't it be incredible if you could find your grandfather?"

"Hannah, you have to realize that not everybody had a wise, compassionate grandfather like you did. I can't imagine that mine is still alive, but even if he is, he definitely wouldn't fall into that category."

"But he—" She hesitated. What could she say about Samuel without revealing that she knew him? "He's your grandfather," she said lamely, knowing only too well that a family connection didn't always mean anything. "I understand that you think he made a big mistake, but surely being descended from him, having his blood in your veins counts for something."

Clayton shook his head slowly and firmly. "Not out here. In this part of the country, every person stands or falls on his own abilities, his own actions. I give my grandfather credit for building this place. But he gave it up. He walked away when things got tough."

"Losing his son and his wife would be enough to break most people."

"You're right. Most people don't belong out here. My grandfather didn't have the extra helping of grit that it takes to make it." Clayton shifted, crossing one ankle over his knee, his expression downgrading to grim. "Even if he thought he could survive this place, he had no right to force it on other people. This ranch killed my father. My parents were making plans to move to town when my father's horse saw a snake, reared up and threw him. He hit his head on a rock. The hospital in town was too far. He didn't make it."

"So your mom really hated it then," she said, encouraging him to continue. This talking business wasn't so hard when you were trying to pry information out of somebody.

He nodded. "Then my grandmother's weak heart gave out from the shock of losing her son. She died, and my grandfather, honorable man that he was, took off for parts unknown. Mom didn't know the first thing about ranching, but there she was—a widow, alone, scared and pregnant with this ranch her only source of income."

She wanted to tell Clayton that Samuel hadn't realized his daughter-in-law was pregnant, that for two years he didn't remember her or even his own name. After that, he'd assumed she'd gone home to her family and the state had taken the ranch.

But she couldn't say any of that.

"Obviously your mother learned how to manage, so it wasn't a total loss." Weak, but it was the best she could come up with at the moment.

Clayton grimaced. "She didn't learn. All she did was hang on until I was old enough to take over. My mother never stood a chance. That was one more reason she wanted me to find another profession. She knew she was losing the ranch. My grandfather may have built this place, but the only reason I still have it is because I've worked damn hard."

"What do you mean, *she was losing the ranch?*"

"My mother had no business trying to manage a place like this." His features were expressionless, his voice a monotone. "She had it practically in bankruptcy when I took over."

"Oh. Oh, dear." Samuel had assumed his ranch had been continuously successful. She could better understand why Clayton resented his grandfather. "But you don't sound like you blame your mother."

"Of course not. She did the best she could."

"Exactly. That's all you can expect from a person. Do you fault your grandmother for dying?"

Clayton blinked and scowled. "What are you talking about?"

"You said your father's death gave your grandmother a heart attack and she died. Do you blame her for that, for not being strong enough to survive?"

"Of course not."

"Then how can you be angry with your grandfather's actions when he lost his son and his wife, when he did the best he could?"

Clayton raked a hand through his hair and studied Hannah. She came up with the damnedest things and somehow made them sound completely logical. "I blame my grandfather for bringing my grandmother out here when she wasn't strong enough to withstand things like losing her son to this harsh land."

She frowned. "That's illogical. I'll bet plenty of the people who live out here have families."

"And most of the women are tough."

"What if you fall in love with somebody who isn't tough? What do you do then?"

Her dark, luminous gaze held his as her words sent a thousand images swirling through his brain.

She was using *you* as a term for *anybody*, he told

himself. She didn't mean *him* specifically. She wasn't
talking about the possibility of his falling in love with
her. That had never entered her mind just as it had
never entered his. So what if her kiss had taken him
on a wild bronc ride up to the sky? They were two
adults with normal, healthy desires. That's all.

"You don't," he said, amazed to hear his voice
sound like a croaking frog. "A man with enough
sense to survive out here has enough sense not to fall
in love with a woman who can't."

"Oh." Her lips surrounded the word, parting
slightly, as if in readiness to be kissed.

Clayton shot to his feet. What the hell was the matter with him? A two-letter word that seemed to be
one of her favorites, and it made him think about
kissing her?

She looked up at him, startled.

"Good night," he said. Good grief! He was beginning to sound like her, saying things out of context.
"I mean, I need to get to bed. Tomorrow's an early
morning. All the mornings are early." Damn! That
was worse. "We'll be up and out about five-thirty,"
he went on, unable to stop himself, "then come back
for breakfast around seven. We work hard, so we eat
big breakfasts." At least he was getting around to
something relevant. "Plenty of strong, black coffee,
a couple of eggs each, a couple of pounds of sausage,
two dozen biscuits, lots of hash browns and a pan full
of gravy."

Her eyes got wider at each item of food. By the
time he reached *gravy,* he expected her to bolt out
the door and drive away as she had yesterday when
he'd offered her this job.

Instead she swallowed hard and nodded, and Clayton was astonished at the wave of relief that washed over him. He'd set out to fire her and, instead, he was relieved she wasn't going to quit.

Heaven help him, he didn't want her to leave. He wanted to try again to teach her to dance. He wanted to hold her slim body against him, smell the scent of roses and feel her soft skin beneath his fingers.

Normal, healthy desires? More like totally out of control.

"Well, I'll see you in the morning, then." He stood, anxious to get his body upstairs and asleep before it did anything dumb.

She nodded once more, rising from her precarious perch on the edge of the chair. "I'll clean up the vase."

"I forgot about that. I'll help." *Good idea,* that little voice taunted, *since she wouldn't have knocked over the table if you'd been able to keep your hands off her.*

He followed Hannah through the dining room.

"Oh, no!"

Her anguished exclamation struck fear in his heart. What now?

He followed her gaze downward, to the bottom of the kitchen door, to the soap bubbles oozing through.

"Hannah, what was it about the dishwasher that you had to figure out?" Clayton asked, trying very hard to keep his voice even. Hannah looked as though she might burst into tears at any minute, and he had no idea what he'd do if that happened. "I know we were running low on dishwasher detergent. You didn't use dishwashing liquid, did you?"

Hannah looked at him indignantly. "Of course not. I know that makes too many suds. But I found some laundry detergent that looked exactly the same as the dishwasher detergent I used for the lunch dishes. I checked carefully, and the laundry soap said it was low-sudsing and had no phosphates and only biodegradable surfactants. It sounded even better for washing items you eat from than the other compound did."

"I see." He didn't, of course. If Hannah was half as confused as she had him, no wonder she kept making a mess of everything she touched. "I suppose we'd better open the door and see how bad it is."

"You go to bed. I'll clean up. It's my fault."

"I insist on helping."

Go upstairs to bed and leave her down here alone, cleaning up? If he did, by some miracle, manage to fall asleep, he'd have nightmares all night.

To think, just minutes ago she'd wanted to leave, and he'd talked her out of it.

And he was still glad he had.

Her insanity was obviously contagious.

He eased the door open, peering cautiously around, fully expecting to be overwhelmed by a mountain of soap bubbles reaching to the ceiling.

"It's not so bad," he assured her, swinging the door wide. The floor was pretty much covered, but only with one layer.

"It's bad," she said glumly.

"The worst is over. See? It's not coming out of the dishwasher anymore. We'll just clean this up, and it's all finished. No big deal." They stood silently, side by side, as the foam oozed over their feet.

"How?" she finally asked.

"I thought you might be able to tell me."

She took a deep breath. "The vacuum is probably out. It would get the bag wet. Anyway, it's not a good

idea to mix water with electrical appliances. We could
sweep up some of it with the broom, but I'm pretty
sure the dustpan doesn't have side panels to contain
the liquid. I suppose we could treat it like an over-
sized spill and sponge it up with towels."

"I suppose we could." She sure knew how to in-
spire confidence in her abilities, he thought sarcastically, then wanted to bite his tongue for thinking
something that sounded like the garbage she'd gotten
from her parents. "I'll go get some old towels," he
said, turning to go.

Her light touch on his arm stopped him, drawing
him back to her, speeding up his heart rate, making
him forget that she had made another mess. She
looked at him for an instant, the same awareness
sparking in her fathomless eyes, then jerked her hand
away and dropped her gaze.

"Your boots," she said breathlessly. "Take off
your boots. They're wet. You'll get soap on the rug."

She was right. Hannah had noticed a potential
problem and taken steps to stop it.

He gave himself a mental slap for the satisfied feeling that came with that thought. The fact that she'd
noticed he was about to worsen the situation she'd
created in the first place didn't mean she'd suddenly
become competent.

"Thanks," he mumbled, then flopped onto a dry
section of the floor and began to work off one boot.

Hannah joined him on the floor, easily slipping off
her canvas shoes to expose slim, smooth, ivory-
skinned feet, then watched his grunting, straining efforts curiously. "Are your boots too small?" she
asked.

"No," he snapped, immediately regretting his tone.

He wasn't upset with her. He was irritated with himself, with his crazy feelings for her, his attraction even to her bare feet. "I have a high instep. It's hard to get my boots on and off. I keep a bootjack upstairs."

"Oh."

He finally got the first one off and removed his sock. She leaned closer, lifting his bare foot with the heel in one hand, studying it as if it held the secrets of the universe. She looked at the boot, then slid the fingers of her other hand along his instep, smoothing his foot and toes into a straight diagonal.

He sat rigid and unmoving...except for his heart, which had started to pound wildly again, and his blood, which had decided to have races between the red and white cells with the winners going straight to his groin. How come he'd never before noticed how sensitive feet could be?

"Could I help?" she asked.

"Help?" he gurgled, an image filling his head of what she might do to help. *That's not what she meant!*

"I could exert leverage from a different angle, and if you hold your foot like this, it should slide out much easier."

He cleared his throat. "That might work, but it'll still take some muscle." More muscle than she had in her slender fingers.

She set his foot on the floor, cupped the bootheel of the other in her hands and stood. No way was he going to tell her that the conventional method for assisting was for her to straddle his leg, take his foot in both hands and pull.

"Okay," she said, "lean back, tilt your foot, straighten your toes."

To his surprise, she managed to wiggle the boot off with a minimum of effort.

"Thanks," he said, grabbing his boots and running upstairs before she decided to study the anatomy of his foot again and cause him to thoroughly embarrass himself by the actions of other portions of his anatomy.

From the linen closet he yanked an armload of old towels. At the same moment he heard a loud thud from the floor below.

Fearing the worst, though unable to even conceive of what that might be, he raced down to find Hannah sprawled in the midst of the bubbles.

"Be careful," she called as he charged into the room and both bare feet slid in different directions, landing him beside her.

"It's slippery," she said apologetically.

Clayton lifted one hand and tried to wipe the slime onto a towel. "Yes," he agreed, "it is."

He wanted to upbraid her for being so careless, for letting him be so careless...for somehow managing to look sensuous sprawled on the floor in the midst of the soapy flood created by her, for making him want to slide his slippery hands over her slippery body.

Instead he felt laughter spill from his lips... hysterical laughter. But anything was preferable to the alternatives—shouting at Hannah and bringing pain to those large, vulnerable eyes or pulling her into his arms, knowing she couldn't possibly fall this time since she was already on the floor.

She looked at him as if he were the one who was insane.

He sobered.

"It's no big deal," he said, amazed to find himself excusing her latest catastrophe, and all because something about her neutralized his common sense, made him act in totally irrational ways.

This wasn't good.

Okay, it felt good...damn good, but it wasn't good. Touching Hannah, kissing her, even *wanting* to touch and kiss her, all held the potential for a much bigger disaster than flooding the floor or breaking a vase.

"Here," he mumbled, "grab a towel, and we'll just sponge it up." She scooted closer to him and reached for the towel he extended toward her, her fingers brushing his, her startled gaze lifting to his.

The back door opened, and she jerked away.

Clayton looked up to see Dub with one hand on the knob, one foot in the kitchen and a startled look on his face. Bear, Mugger, Cruiser and Bob crowded close behind.

"Uh, hi, Boss," Dub said. "We didn't mean to interrupt anything. We figured you were already in bed by now, and we, uh, just thought we might have a little snack. Like we always do. It's our little routine before we go to bed. Sorry we bothered you." Shoving everybody backward, Dub closed the door behind them.

Dub was lying. They'd never come in for snacks when Mrs. Grogan was there. They were here now because Hannah's meal had been so terrible.

Everybody, including himself, was lying to protect Hannah, to keep from hurting her sensitive feelings, to avoid telling her she had no business out here where only the strong survive and that she'd better run home as fast as she could.

Well, nobody was doing her any favors by not tell-

ing her the truth. It was up to him. He'd tell her right
now. Get it over with. Do the best thing for everybody.

He looked at her sitting cross-legged beside him,
her clothes soggy, her head dipping to allow her ram-
pant curls to fall over her face, her white-knuckled
fingers clutching an old green towel, every part of her
body retreating from failure. She knew the guys
weren't being honest.

Brushing her hair back, he tilted her chin to force
her to look at him.

"They don't usually come back for snacks, do
they?" she asked softly.

"Of course they do!" he protested, fighting a sudden, compelling urge to plant feathery kisses on her
eyelids, her cheeks, her smooth white neck. Kiss her
until she lost that sad look, until desire was the only
thing he could see in those wide, deep eyes.

Abruptly he dropped her chin and scrambled to his
feet—not an easy task in the slime. What had happened to his resolution to be honest with her?

He tossed a towel onto the floor and began to mop.
"Every evening they come in about this time and
make sandwiches and eat cookies and pie and drink
all the milk and anything they can find." He touched
a finger to his nose to see if it had grown any. It did
seem a little longer than he'd noticed before.

Tomorrow, he promised himself. For Hannah's
own good, tomorrow he'd figure out a way to fire her.

She slid up to the kitchen sink at the same time he
did, both clutching sodden towels to wring out. His
arm touched hers. That's all. An accidental brushing
of flesh against flesh, but it might as well have been

his hand on her breast, on her thigh, so intimate was the sensation.

That wasn't the kind of fire he'd meant!

Chapter Seven

Five-thirty in the morning was not a decent hour for a human to be up and about, Hannah decided as she staggered into Clayton's kitchen to wrestle with filling his breakfast order.

She'd been rudely awakened at the unnatural hour by the sound of Clayton's boots going down the uncarpeted hallway and stairs. She suspected he stomped extra hard to make sure she got up.

Probably just as well. The noise had interrupted a dream gone bad, a dream about him. They were dancing, waltzing round and round like the figurines on a music box, and she felt graceful and elegant. Then he'd bent to kiss her.

Her lips tingled as she waited...but a clap of thunder had shaken the floor and she tripped and fell, hitting him in the eye with her elbow and splashing soap bubbles all over him.

Too close to reality. Of course Clayton hadn't paid any attention to her weak attempts to reconcile him

with his grandfather. Why should he listen to someone who fed him fried toothpicks, stepped on his feet
when he kissed her then stumbled and broke a family
heirloom? Someone who couldn't do anything right.

And why had her brain—the one thing she'd always been able to count on—deserted her and let her
become attracted to a man who expected perfection?
Well, if not perfection, at least expected her to cook
and dance.

Even if he knew the truth, Hannah had already discovered that computer programming wasn't the kind
of talent that ranked her high on anyone's party in-
vitation list. Somehow she couldn't quite imagine
Clayton getting all dreamy-eyed over her ability to
put a computer through its paces. She was certain
showing him one of her programs would not produce
the same reaction as their brief, ill-fated dance had.

She sighed and opened the refrigerator door from
habit. Of course there were none of the familiar red
cans of cola that greeted her at home each morning
with their eye-opening blend of caffeine, sugar and
effervescence.

If she'd gone home last night the way she wanted
to, she could be safe in her own cozy apartment right
now, opening the refrigerator to a supply of cold cola.

She yawned and closed the refrigerator door.

Actually, if she were at home, she'd still be sound
asleep.

Why had she let Clayton talk her out of leaving
last night? In the same mystifying vein, why *had* he
talked her out of leaving?

She could understand her own lapse better than
Clayton's. She hated to admit defeat.

And in spite of his attitude toward his grandfather,

she liked Clayton, admired him, in fact. If nothing else, she admired the way he could walk across the room without tripping. He could dance. He could kiss.

Oh, my, could he kiss.

He could manage a huge ranch. He could hold his life together all on his own.

His skills at hiring an experienced housekeeper needed to be reprogrammed, but he had been pretty much forced into that situation by Samuel's banker.

Even in the way he walked, Clayton exhibited confidence. He'd always been a success, and he wouldn't have much patience with someone who wasn't. Someone like her.

Which made his failure to send her packing after yesterday's events even more puzzling.

What she needed to do was focus on her mission and get out before Clayton got her head and her hormones any more confused.

She needed to call Samuel and talk to him—not about her absurd reaction to Clayton, but about Clayton's attitude toward his grandfather. Samuel claimed to be an early riser. She'd see just how early he meant.

She went into the living room and dialed his number, but got his answering machine.

Her heart fluttered erratically as memories bombarded her of the day she'd called her grandfather and he hadn't answered the phone. She'd called all day before she finally went over to his house to check on him and found that he'd died in his sleep.

She took a deep breath and ordered herself to be rational. Samuel was probably in the shower or still asleep and didn't hear the phone. She left a brief message telling him she'd call later, then returned to the kitchen.

Clayton had threatened her last night with a seven o'clock return of the hungry troops.

Thank goodness she could program computers and didn't have to do something as complicated, time-consuming and imprecise as cooking on a regular basis.

Clayton squinted into the rising sun. Not a cloud in the sky. About as much chance of rain today as he had of getting a decent breakfast this morning.

At least Hannah should be awake. As he'd passed her room on the way out, he'd paused at her door, listening for sounds of activity, needing to know if she was still there or if she'd disappeared into the night after the disaster with the dishwasher.

When he hadn't heard any sounds, he'd opened the door a crack to peek inside. The relief he felt at seeing her sleeping form was totally inexplicable. But that hadn't been the only emotion she'd stirred in him. Looking innocent and vulnerable, she lay on her back, one arm draped over the white eyelet bedspread. She wore something light colored and nondescript. Probably a T-shirt. Nothing deliberately sexy or alluring, but somehow it was.

The predawn shadows brushed her face with a sensuous look. As he watched, her lips parted slowly, enticingly, as if she was waiting to be kissed. He thought she gave a soft moan.

When he realized his own lips had parted in response, he immediately closed the door, then stood in the hallway wondering if he'd imagined the entire scene. From Hannah's sleeping form in a dark room, he'd created a tantalizing fantasy.

He backed away from the door, from Hannah, from his own crazy libido, and stomped down the hall and out of the house. The noise would serve to wake Hannah, he'd told himself. But mostly he'd stomped from frustration. Fixating on a fragile woman who was a continuing catastrophe was the last thing he needed to do right now.

The ranch demanded all his time and attention, and that was the way he wanted it. So what if Hannah could send him into orbit? So what if her guileless approach to life touched something deep inside?

Guileless and helpless, he reminded himself.

This country had a way of getting rid of helpless people. The grandfather Hannah wanted so badly for him to forgive, his grandmother, his mother, his father.

Only he and the ranch always remained. Those were the only two he dared count on.

"Boss? Clay?"

The words filtered into Clayton's consciousness. He blinked and looked over to see that Dub had ridden up beside him.

The cowhand laughed. "Man, you were sure off in another world."

"Yeah, I got a lot on my mind."

Dub nodded understandingly. "We don't get some rain pretty soon, even the cacti are gonna dry up and blow away."

Clayton scanned the desolate landscape. "I'm afraid we're going to have burn pear again in the next day or two." Burning the spines off the cacti would allow the cattle to eat them and gain nourishment as

well as water, but it was a tedious, time-consuming
process. And they'd already done it once, during the
winter when the lack of rain had made the winter
grass crop almost nonexistent.

"That's what I come to talk to you about," Dub
said. "We found a calf this morning that's probably
going to have to go on a bottle. Him and his mama
both look pretty scrawny."

Clayton cursed as he tugged on the reins and turned
his horse. "Let's go take a look at the little fellow
then head on in for some breakfast."

"Uh, what do you reckon the new cook is gonna
make for breakfast?"

"Oh, the usual." Clayton tried to sound nonchalant
and confident, as if he really believed anything Hannah did would be *usual*. Privately he thought he might
be up for some of that prickly pear cactus instead.

"Look!" Dub exclaimed, pointing.

A large, dark creature lumbered across their path,
quills swaying with the motion of his body.

"I'll be damned," Clayton said. "It *is* a porcupine.
You don't see them around here very often. He'll be
gone before long. The pickings are too slim."

"Looks pretty fat and sassy to me." Dub clucked
to his horse and rode around the unconcerned creature.

When they got to the corral, Cruiser was already
feeding the little calf from a bottle. It looked to be
several days old, but it was weak and shaky. Cruiser
kept one hand under its stomach, helping it to stand.

A range cow imprisoned in a chute nearby bawled
mournfully.

"She don't much like the idea of me taking over
with her baby," Cruiser said, smiling up at Clayton.

"Guess it upsets her 'cause she can't take care of him."

"I don't blame her for that." In fact, it further endeared the half-wild creature to him. She took her responsibilities seriously. She'd never leave the calf to fend for himself. She was below optimum weight, no excess body fat, nothing she could spare for her baby. Yet she gave her offspring all she could.

"It's okay, Mama," he said in a soothing voice, guiding his horse over to the distraught cow. "I'll take care of your baby and you, too." The cow's eyes rolled and she gave another pitiful bawl.

After breakfast he would put Bob and Mugger to burning pear. And he might as well figure on buying another load of hay. The cattle had to eat properly.

If this drought kept up, he might as well figure on not being able to pay off the mortgage and maybe even being forced to ask for an extension, he reflected grimly.

He tugged on the reins and turned his horse, refusing to dwell on that possibility. It would be a minor setback, not the end of the world. Nothing like the problems he'd had to face nine years ago when he'd taken over.

But it still irritated him. He'd planned to have the ranch free and clear this year. Failure to do so would be just that...failure.

He looked up at the cloudless sky and tried to ignore the thought of his dwindling bank account.

"Let's go get some breakfast, guys."

As they rode up to the house, Clayton saw Hannah standing on the front porch gazing toward the sun. At first glance she seemed to be a strong, willowy pioneer woman bending into the wind in her ankle-

length, flowing dress. For a brief moment he was a
cowboy a hundred years ago returning to his woman
after a hard trail ride, to the warm, comfortable home
she kept for him.

He shook his head to dispel the outrageous
thoughts. Hannah wasn't strong, and he doubted that
she'd made the house comfortable. He supposed it
could be *warm*. She might have set it on fire.

As he got closer, he noticed that Hannah was covered from head to foot with flour, her white-streaked
hair in wild disarray. What had happened? Had the
flour bin exploded?

He urged his horse to a gallop.

She turned toward the sound, and the wind blew a
tangle of the pasty curls across her face.

Clayton reined to a halt in front of the porch and
swung down. "What's the matter?" He strode onto
the porch and took her arm. "Are you hurt? Did
something blow up?"

She pushed her hair back, and her tentative smile
turned to a hurt frown. "I made breakfast," she said,
then spun away from him and disappeared into the
house.

"What'd you do to her?" Dub demanded, riding
up to the porch.

Clayton drew a hand across his forehead and
sighed, amazed and dismayed at how relieved he was
that she was all right. He had neither the time nor the
emotional energy to be worrying about the welfare of
a woman who had a major talent for creating worri-
some situations.

"Why'd she run inside like that?" Mugger wanted
to know.

"I guess I hurt her feelings," Clayton replied. "I didn't mean to."

Bob nodded sagely. "She does seem to be a mite skittish. Well, let's go see what kind of critters we're having for breakfast."

Whatever it was, Clayton reflected, he'd better be prepared to eat it and grin after upsetting Hannah the way he had.

For a fleeting moment he wondered what had happened to his insistence on competency from employees. His hormones must have drowned it.

He followed the boys inside.

The coffee tasted like sludge, the scrambled eggs were tough, the hash browns gray and gummy, the sausage black, the gravy could be cut with a knife and eaten with a fork, and the leftover biscuits could be used for skeet shooting.

The guys covered everything with picante sauce and ate as though their taste buds had ceased to function. Bear even asked for seconds. Maybe he was afraid she'd recycle it for lunch if he didn't finish it.

Maybe they were all as hungry as that poor cow who'd be eating prickly pear cactus just as soon as somebody burned off the thorns.

Clayton thought Hannah seemed to be a little more relaxed, only in the beginning stages of a nervous breakdown instead of far advanced. Every time the men said something to her, she'd look startled, then smile shyly and blush. Sometimes she'd even laugh softly. The guys must have liked her reaction. They were practically vying to talk to her, each comment becoming more ridiculous than the last—Texas tall tales.

"I come across a twelve-foot rattle snake last sum-

mer," Bear drawled. "His fangs was six inches long.
Scared me, I got to admit. I started talking real fast,
telling him all about our president and congress and
all that stuff, and pretty soon that old snake opened
his mouth big enough to swallow a good-size calf. I
figured I was done for, but that old snake was so
bored, he was yawning. By the time I got to the gov-
ernor, he was snoring. Slept so hard I pulled out both
fangs and stuck his own rattles in his mouth. Then I
yelled at him. That old snake woke up, lunged for me
and commenced to roll like a hoop. Probably ended
up in the Gulf of Mexico."

Hannah laughed, her eyes shining and pink flooding her cheeks. It was like the sunrise Clayton had
just seen...brilliant splashes of color rising from the
dark horizon, spreading and glowing to light the entire sky.

She never looked directly at him. Of course, he
wasn't contributing any tall tales. He was concentrating on getting through breakfast without losing a
tooth on the biscuits or a filling in the hash browns.

Anyway, he was the boss. He was in charge. He
had to figure out how to hold things together. He
couldn't afford to waste time being silly.

If Hannah didn't look at him and smile, that was
perfectly all right. Just fine. No problem.

He stood and shoved back his chair. "You boys
ready to get on with work? We've got a lot to do
today, especially if we're going to burn pear."

Hannah looked at him then, and he hated himself
for the flush of happiness that washed over him.

"Burn pear?" she repeated, but before he could
explain, Bob jumped in, then Cruiser had to tell her
about the calf he'd been bottle-feeding.

"Did you get the milk from another cow?" she asked, her attention diverted from him again.

"Oh, no, ma'am," Dub said. "You don't milk range cows like you do dairy cows. They're wild animals. Anyway, they're all in about as bad a shape as this one's mama. Doing all they can to feed their own calves. We got powdered formula down at the barn. Just mix it up like you would for a real baby."

"Want to come watch?" Mugger invited.

"She won't have time unless you don't want her to cook lunch," Clayton snapped, then realized that threat didn't really have any teeth to it. "Or if you don't want your laundry done."

Hannah's head jerked back around to him, her eyes expanding in horror.

Oh, no! Surely she could do laundry.

She averted her gaze, looked down at the table, and began to gather up the dirty dishes.

The cowboys moved away, heading outside to get on with their work. Clayton stood rooted to the spot, paralyzed by a combination of inexplicable fascination with Hannah's every movement and fear of what she planned to do with those dishes.

"Don't forget to call the grocery store and order some more dishwasher detergent," he said as soon as he heard the front door slam behind the men.

Her arms precariously full of picante-streaked dishes, she looked up. A gamut of emotions from hurt to determination flashed across her expressive face. She lifted her chin. "I know."

"You probably need a lot of other things, too. Maybe I'd better stay a little while and help you decide what to order."

"I can do it," she said, but she didn't sound very confident.

They stared at each other across the table as the full import of Clayton's dilemma sank in. If he didn't stay, he couldn't even imagine what she might order from the grocery store. If he did stay, he could stand beside her, shoulder to shoulder, thigh to thigh, cheek to cheek, while they checked the pantry and the freezer and made up a list together.

He liked the latter idea entirely too much. The image sent his blood rushing. He'd already determined that close proximity to Hannah switched his libido on and his common sense off.

"You get started on the laundry," he suggested, "while I make a list, then you can add whatever you want after I leave." He gave himself a mental pat on the back for that idea even while he fought down the disappointment.

This would give him a chance to see that Hannah had the necessities to cook with no matter how she chose to mutilate them. Not only that, but he could also be sure she wasn't going to do something bizarre with the laundry, like add detergent to the dryer.

She nodded, then turned and went into the kitchen, dribbling silverware behind her.

She was the embodiment of chaos and incompetence. And no way was he going after her to pull her into his arms and cause her to drop the rest of the dishes and kiss her until they both forgot the mess around them. Absolutely no way. He wasn't even considering it.

Hannah carried the dirty dishes into the kitchen and set what she hadn't dropped onto the counter. Just when she'd been so pleased with herself for beginning to comprehend the structure of this cooking thing, Clayton not only wanted her to do laundry, but he made it quite clear that he didn't trust her to compile her own grocery list.

Not that she trusted herself to do it, but Clayton had no reason to think she couldn't after she'd cooked her best meal yet. Okay, the food still wasn't edible, but it was an improvement. The coffee, at least, had looked okay. Since she didn't drink the stuff herself, she had no way of being certain, but nobody had put picante sauce in it.

She went from the kitchen into the laundry room. When she'd come in to get meat from the freezer, she'd noticed the assortment of bags ranging from canvas to pillowcases, all stuffed to bursting with lumpy items of some sort. Curious array but she hadn't wanted to pry. This must be, she deduced, the laundry she was supposed to wash.

Other than the fact that there was a lot of it, this wouldn't be any different from doing her own. She could handle it. Clayton wouldn't be able to find fault with her performance on this.

She walked over and peeked inside one of the bags, then drew back in horror.

Underwear. Red with black polka dots, purple with green swirls, tiger-striped...

How would she ever be able to look those cowboys in the face again knowing what kind of underwear one of them was wearing?

It could even belong to Clayton. Last night when he'd pressed against her—

No! She couldn't possibly tell anything about his underwear from that.

"Find everything all right?"

She whirled to see Clayton standing in the doorway, one arm lifted, his hand resting on the frame. Try as she might to focus on his face, her gaze darted downward. She couldn't pull her eyes away, couldn't stop herself from imagining him in a pair of tiger-striped shorts.

"Yes," she said, but the giggle that erupted from her throat at the same time garbled the word. She opened another bag and immediately recognized the scent of leather and hard work as belonging to Clayton. Thank goodness! That meant the underwear belonged to somebody else.

Gratefully she yanked out the first item. Blue jeans. Stained blue jeans. She could handle stained blue jeans. She'd show Clayton she could do this right.

She threw them onto the washing machine and opened the cabinet above. Prespotter. A larger container than she had at home and lacking the handy spray nozzle, but she knew what to do with it.

She poured some onto a large black stain. She couldn't find a used tooth brush, but she did see the handle of a larger brush. Using that, she scrubbed the area, then repeated the process until she'd prespotted every stain. With a flourish she tossed the jeans into the washer and, as if drawn by a physical force, turned to look at Clayton, to get his reaction...his approval.

His expression was intense. Whatever he was thinking, he was thinking it hard and deep, but he stood erect and turned away before she could figure it out.

"You'll probably need to use bleach for the kind of dirt we get around here," he said just before the door closed behind him.

Bleach. Oh, yes. She'd heard of using bleach for really discolored areas.

She took down the large plastic container. Apparently they used a lot of it here. The bottle was almost empty. But she saw another full one behind it.

She poured some onto the first stain and scrubbed. Clayton had emphasized how tough the stains were. Maybe she ought to add a little extra. She started to turn on the machine, then hesitated.

When she'd spilled blackberry jam on her yellow blouse, Mrs. Henson had soaked the stain for a long time before it finally came out.

She'd better let all the clothes set for twenty or thirty minutes before washing them.

By gosh, this was one thing Clayton wouldn't be able to find fault with. She *would* get those spots out.

Chapter Eight

Find recipes for lunch and dinner. Call the grocery store to place an order. Set meat out to thaw for lunch and dinner. Take a shower and scrub the dried biscuit dough out of her hair.

Good grief! Hannah would never again complain about a tight deadline for one of her programs. How incredibly relaxing it would be to have nothing to think about except the movements of computerized unicorns and dragons, how to structure a system of points and how to tell the computer to do it.

She put a package of still frozen hamburger meat into the oven to make a meatloaf for lunch. It was bound to thaw more quickly in there than on the counter. Those little bits of white paper she hadn't been able to get off would surely come loose when it warmed a bit.

She went back to the living room and called Samuel a second time. Still no answer.

Which didn't mean a thing, she assured herself as

she stood listening to the twelfth ring. He could be any number of places. This whole situation was stressing her totally. She needed a "fix" of tranquility. She needed her computer. She should have brought her laptop, but she'd had no intention of staying here long enough to need it.

However, Clayton had a computer upstairs, a dusty computer he apparently never used. It wouldn't have the programs she needed, of course, but she could use the modem to tap into her home computer, which she always left on, or to get data off the Net.

Surely he wouldn't mind if she took a short break. She already had lunch thawing in the oven and clothes in the washing machine.

She went upstairs.

As she settled in at Clayton's desk, she felt a twinge of guilt for using someone else's equipment without asking, but Clayton wasn't there to ask and, anyway, the machine had her accounting program on it. That surely gave her some kind of user's rights. In the picture above the desk, a young Samuel smiled down benignly as if giving his blessing.

All guilt soon vanished in the comfortable, safe world of bytes and RAM.

When she made an attempt to access her own computer, Hannah discovered that Clayton hadn't hooked up his modem. No problem. Since it was internal, all she had to do was plug it into the phone line.

She turned off the computer then found the connecting cable still in the box in the corner.

With its wide overhang, the desk sat a few inches away from the back wall so she had no problem plugging the modem cord into the computer. Tracing the phone line to the wall entry in the far corner where the other end of the cord needed to be connected, however, was a more complicated matter.

The only way she could see to get to the wall jack was to go behind the desk. She was barely able to wriggle through the opening then move her shoulders into the space under the desk and reach under and up on the other end.

She sneezed as the dust she'd disturbed settled in her nose. So much for Mrs. Grogan's housekeeping skills. How odd that someone would choose to keep the kitchen clean and not the computer room. Some people had the oddest priorities.

With two fingers she managed to wiggle out the plastic tab from the phone line, then crawl out to plug it into the computer and back under to plug the computer into the wall. What had Clayton been thinking when he'd shoved his desk into the corner against the phone jack like that?

Getting the line in was more difficult than getting it out had been. She couldn't get the blasted thing centered in the small amount of space, and her dusty fingers were becoming damp with perspiration from the frustration.

Through her haze of concentration, she barely heard the door close.

Footsteps crossed the room, and Hannah froze. Even without twisting around to look from under the desk, she knew Clayton had entered the room. His scent of leather, horses and earth drifted to her through the dust. The confident walk belonged to him, and something else, something intangible that tingled all her senses, told her Clayton was near.

And she was scrunched up under his desk, trying

to plug in his computer modem. She didn't think this was likely to increase his confidence in her.

Couldn't she get anything right?

Maybe he was just looking for an invoice or something, and he'd leave before he discovered her.

More likely he'd remember a favorite dustbunny he used to play with as a boy and choose this moment to look under the desk for it.

She held her breath and scrunched up against the wall as tightly as possible.

The chair scooted across the wooden floor. She flinched. No desk pad. He'd ruin the floor. He definitely needed some help getting his office together.

As if he'd listen to anything she suggested, especially if he caught her now.

She heard him flop into the chair then a clicking noise. More clicking noises.

The phone! He was trying to get a dial tone. And she'd messed it up.

Panic making her clumsy fingers even clumsier, Hannah fumbled frantically, pushing the jack into the outlet.

The faint sound of beeps told her she must have succeeded. He was dialing a number.

Then he cursed, and the clicking began again.

Hannah repositioned the jack and pushed. She couldn't tell if it clicked in or not, but decided this wasn't a good time to test it. She kept her shaking fingers pressed against the plastic, holding it in place.

Clayton's phone call apparently went through.

"Frank, this is Clayton Sinclair.... Fine, how about you all...? Good, good. Listen, I need another load of hay.... Good God, man, that's almost double what you charged me for the last one...! I know, I know.

You're hurting from the drought, too. We all are. How soon can you get it here...? Good. I'll have a check waiting for you."

He hung up, and Hannah relaxed her grip on the phone jack. She hadn't ruined his call, and he hadn't caught her—yet.

Then she heard a faint click. Oh, no! He was going to make another call. She pushed on the jack again and prayed this one would be as impersonal as the last. What would she do if he called a girlfriend or someone really personal? Where was a time-space continuum warp when you really needed one?

"Glen? This is Clayton."

Glen? That could be a woman or a man!

"Things are a little tight right now, Glen."

And Clayton's voice was one of those things. Whatever he had to say to Glen, he wasn't happy about saying it.

"I may have to ask for an extension on the mortgage loan."

His banker. He was talking to his banker. Thank goodness.

In spite of a nagging guilt over listening to someone's financial affairs, Hannah found herself fascinated by his distress as he went on. It was, after all, only a business deal. He was asking for an extension of a loan, not giving up his soul.

Clayton sighed, long and hard. "That's fine," he said, contradicting his sigh and his tone. "Work up some figures, and I'll get back to you as soon as I have something definite on this end."

Again Clayton hung up.

Please leave and go back to wrestling cattle or

rustling them or whatever! Hannah willed him silently.

The chair creaked as if he were leaning back in it. Hannah ignored the itch that suddenly sprang up behind her right shoulder blade.

"One of these days I'm going to wipe that smirk off your face, Samuel Sinclair," Clayton said quietly.

Samuel was here?

"It's easy enough to smile and look superior when you're sitting up there in a frame, when you don't have to deal with life."

He was talking to Samuel's picture. She frequently talked to her grandfather's picture, but the tone wasn't quite the same.

"It gets tough down here in the real world, but I can handle it. I didn't need you around after all. As soon as I get the mortgage paid off, we're square, you and me, and you're out of here."

This didn't bode at all well for a reconciliation.

"If I didn't know better," Clayton continued, still in the same deadly calm voice, "I'd think you somehow arranged for all this—the drought, the low cattle prices...my new housekeeper."

Hannah's heart clenched painfully. He put her in the same category as drought and low cattle prices? Ironically, though, he was right about the fact that Samuel had arranged her appearance in his life.

He chuckled softly. "Or maybe I should say," he went on, his tone changing, lightening, becoming almost whimsical, "my new house*wrecker*."

Housewrecker?

A tickle on her hand, braced against the wall, caught her attention, and she looked to see a spider casually and rather gracefully making his way across her knuckles. She clenched her teeth and tightened every muscle in her body, willing herself not to move. She wasn't afraid of spiders, but she'd never wanted to become this intimate with one, either.

In spite of her determination to hold still and ignore the creature, she flinched, her head hitting the top of the desk, making a noise that sounded like thunder. Her heart sank as any hope of escaping without total humiliation vanished.

The chair slid noisily across the floor and the air pressure in the room seemed to intensify to the point of exploding.

She twisted around, trying to see out into the room...and looked directly into Clayton's eyes.

For a moment neither spoke. She had enough trouble trying to figure out what to say under normal circumstances. She was at a total loss now.

He ran a hand through his hair and shook his head. "Hannah? Is that you?" he finally asked, his voice frustrated but astonishingly calm, all things considered.

However, his tone only worsened Hannah's discomfort. His rational approach accentuated the bizarreness of her position.

"What are you doing under my desk?" he asked when she failed to come up with an answer to his first question.

If she couldn't answer the first one, she wasn't very likely to get this one.

He drew in a deep breath and let it out slowly, resignedly, as if giving up on a logical explanation for her presence. "Do you need some help getting out?"

At last something to which she knew the proper

response. She tried to nod but couldn't move her head that much. "Yes," she managed to say. "Thank you." Always be polite. Wouldn't her mother be pleased to know that her daughter retained *some* of the social graces?

He leaned forward, grasped her shoulders and tugged. She didn't budge.

"How did you get under there?"

"I came through the back."

He stood, circled the desk and picked up her feet. Her size nine, clumsy feet clad in worn canvas shoes. With any luck, she'd die of humiliation and he'd haul out only her lifeless body.

"Okay," he said. "You push, and I'll pull."

His hands closed around her ankles. Thank goodness she'd just showered and shaved her legs.

Clayton gave a tug, she gave a shove, and they both sprawled on the floor, her legs up around his shoulders.

Hannah's face burned as she scrambled around, trying to right herself from the suggestive position and only making it worse. With one foot still over his shoulder, she raked her other calf across his nose.

Had anyone ever actually died from embarrassment? She might be the first.

He lifted her legs, his hands warm on her skin—or maybe her legs were blushing as hotly as her face. He seemed to move in slow motion as he extricated himself from her. As soon as her legs lay quietly on the floor, Clayton rose with no apparent effort.

Well, sure, coordinated people could do that.

He reached down, cupping her elbows, and pulled her up to stand in front of him. "Are you all right?" he asked.

She nodded, holding on to his forearms for support. Her legs felt oddly shaky. Probably just from too much time in a cramped position.

He didn't move.

She didn't move.

Clayton gazed down at her, his eyes becoming smoky instead of bright blue. An inexplicable phenomenon. Hannah ordered her gaze to move away from those eyes, and it did—only to come to a precarious halt at his lips. Wide, sensuous lips. The kind of lips movie cameras used for a close-up just before the hot kiss scene.

Clayton yanked his hands away, covered his mouth and sneezed. Five times in rapid succession.

Hannah stepped back. That never happened in the movies. The man was never allergic to the woman.

"You're supposed to use a broom or a vacuum or something besides yourself to dust with," Clayton said when he caught his breath.

Hannah looked down at her dress. She was covered in dust. She started brushing it off, but, in the resulting cloud, Clayton sneezed again.

"I'll go outside to do this." If she got away fast, maybe he'd forget she'd never told him what she'd been doing under his desk in the first place.

Or maybe he really believed she'd been acting as a human duster. After his rude comment about her being a housewrecker, she wouldn't be surprised.

"Good idea." Clayton retrieved his hat from the desk and started after her.

"I can dust myself off," she protested. How incompetent did he think she was? Though the idea of his hands sliding across the fabric of her dress flashed tantalizingly through her demented mind.

Clayton's gaze scanned her from head to toe, but before she could see his expression, he slapped his hat onto his head, the brim low in front. "I know you can," he said. "I'm going with you because I've got to get back to work outside."

"Oh. Of course." She hadn't thought she could be any more embarrassed, but she was.

They went downstairs in silence. At least she'd avoided a confrontation about her position under his desk.

But at the bottom of the stairs, Clayton stopped her with a hand on her arm. His touch was gentle, but she turned slowly to face him, expecting the worst.

He took his hat off and held it in one hand while twirling the brim with the other.

He looked nervous, Hannah realized with astonishment. Was that possible? Was she not the only one who suffered from this affliction? What did he have to be nervous about?

"I guess you overheard me say some things up there."

That was it. He knew she'd heard him putting her on a par with droughts and low cattle prices. She shrugged, unwilling to admit he'd hurt her feelings. "It's okay."

"That picture over my desk is my grandfather, the man you were asking me about last night." A curtain came down to cover Clayton's uncertain expression, and he gazed beyond her, avoiding her eyes or looking at something in the distance she couldn't see.

"When I was a kid, I had to watch helplessly while my mom struggled to keep this place going. I used to talk to that picture up there and beg my grandfather to come home and take care of us." He gave a careless shrug. "Of course he never did. I grew up and wasn't helpless anymore. So I set a goal that by the time I was thirty years old, I'd have this place back the way it was when my grandfather left—the mortgage paid and the herd back to the size it was. I'd erase all the problems he caused by leaving. Then it would be my ranch. It's become kind of a personal battle between the two of us. And I *will* win."

Hannah shook her head slowly. "That's not winning when you lose somebody as special as your grandfather."

"You keep getting our grandfathers confused. Mine was special, all right, but not in the same way yours was." He lifted a hand to her cheek. "Hannah, you're so...so naive. Unworldly. You just don't understand that not everybody's kind and caring."

He took his hand away from her cheek and looked at it as if surprised by its actions, then turned and strode out the door.

She could have laughed at that assessment. She, of all people, knew how unkind others could be, even when they cared.

She followed Clayton outside, intending to get rid of her accumulation of dust.

At the edge of the porch, he turned back.

"Hannah, why were you under my desk?"

Oh, my. He hadn't forgotten.

"I wasn't exactly under it. More like behind it. The under part just happened." She brushed vigorously at her skirt, trying to send the dust in Clayton's direction. Maybe if he started sneezing again...

"All right. So why were you *behind* my desk?"

She faced him squarely. She couldn't lie to him. She'd have to admit she'd been using his computer, then her charade would be over. "The phone jack's at the end of the desk in the corner. It's very hard to reach."

"I know that. But why did you need to reach it? Did the phone come unplugged?" His voice was preternaturally calm, as if he were speaking to a mental patient who might become dangerous at any moment.

"No. I unplugged it."

"I see." He didn't see. She could tell by his tone.

"Your computer modem wasn't connected," she explained.

His eyes widened. "My computer modem? Hannah, I don't think it's a good idea for you to do things to my computer. That's an expensive piece of equipment. It's awfully easy to mess up if you don't know what you're doing."

No kidding! He'd done a pretty good job of messing it up before she came along. "I know computers. Maybe I'm not a great cook or a terrific dancer, but I know computers like...like you know your ranch."

There. It was out in the open. No more pretending. At least he'd realize she was proficient at something even though it certainly wasn't being a housekeeper or dancing or anything even remotely romantic.

"I could help you get set up," she continued bravely. "That computer sitting gathering dust could improve your operations a thousand percent. You could restructure your finances, check cattle futures, hay prices, whatever you need to know to allow you to make the best business decision."

He looked at her curiously for a long moment.

"Hannah, that's really nice of you to want to help. I think it's great that you can use a computer, but I'm afraid it's going to take somebody who's pretty knowledgeable in the field to get me set up. Sometimes when we try to do things we're not really qualified for, we do more harm than good. When things slow down this winter, I'll get somebody from the computer school in San Antonio to come out and help me. Much as I appreciate your offer of help, I think it would be better if you focus on being the best, er, uh, housekeeper you can be and forget about computers."

He smiled encouragingly, swung onto his horse and rode away leaving her standing on the porch in shock.

Anger, hurt and helplessness—all the old feelings—surged through her as she watched him ride away.

He didn't believe her! He was patronizing her, making her feel like an inept adolescent again.

When in fact, she'd already cleaned up the problem he'd created on the computer he didn't want her to touch!

She tried to be rational about the matter. He had justifiable reason to think her assertion of computer expertise might be a bit inflated. After all, she'd presented herself to him as a competent cook and housekeeper, and he'd already noticed that she'd misrepresented herself there.

Nevertheless, a wave of intense yearning swept over her, a desire to be back home, back in her safe world where she was a competent, respected computer programmer. She'd get her clothes and go home right now. Be gone before he returned.

She retreated into the house and headed for her room, but the smell of her hamburger meat stopped her with one foot on the bottom stair. It definitely smelled thawed...and then some. She probably ought to take it out of the oven and make it into a meatloaf.

Bear, Dub, Cruiser, Mugger and Bob deserved to have a good lunch.

She'd better check on the laundry, too. She could leave Clayton's clean clothes on his bed, just a reminder of how unfair he was. She could do some things right.

The hamburger meat was definitely thawed. In fact, the outside part was pretty much cooked. Oh, well. The whole thing had to cook eventually. After she mixed it up with all those other components, who'd ever be able to tell which parts got done first?

The cooked part didn't crumble very easily; it stuck together in solid chunks, but it would probably mush up with the other stuff as it cooked.

She left the meat cooling on the counter and went to put the wash in the dryer. She drew out a denim shirt, then straightened it to see if all the stains were gone.

That was odd. She didn't remember taking any rags out of Clayton's bag. Probably something he used to wipe grease off the tractor or clean the stables. It had certainly come out clean, anyway. What there was of it.

She took out a pair of blue jeans. Tattered and full of holes. She definitely didn't remember those. And Clayton wasn't the *trendy* type.

With a growing sense of panic, she yanked more clothes from the washer.

Nothing but rags. Clean, stain-free rags.

This was not *likely to impress Clayton.*

She sank to the floor in despair, surrounded by Clayton's former clothes.

It was time to give up. For years Hannah had tried to get her parents to see her as something other than a lump of failure. She wasn't going down that road again.

She'd check the tags on Clayton's clothes, order more for him on her charge card, then she was out of here. She had to get away or all the inner peace she'd gained over the past few years would be totally destroyed.

Along with Clayton's ranch.

That last thought produced a half-hysterical giggle.

She'd proved herself the best at something besides computer programming. She was the best darned *housewrecker* around.

The giggle ended on a choked sound that more closely resembled a sob. She definitely had to stop beating her head against the granite wall of Clayton's disapproval.

She gathered up the rags and ran into the living room, snatched up the phone and dialed Samuel's number.

He sounded tired when he answered.

"Did I wake you?" she asked. "Were you still asleep?"

"I was just taking a little nap," he said. "How are things going?"

"Terrible. I'm coming home." Suddenly she had to fight back sad, angry tears. "I'm sorry, but your grandson's a jerk. I don't think you can ever be reconciled with him, and why would you want to, anyway? He's determined to save the ranch to prove to you that he doesn't need you even though he thinks you're dead and he has to ask for an extension on the mortgage and he doesn't want me to touch his computer and I ruined his clothes." She dabbed her eyes with the ragged sleeve of a shirt.

"Hannah, calm down. Tell me what's happened."

A weakness in his voice cut through her self-absorbed anger. "What's wrong? You don't sound right. Where were you when I called earlier this morning?"

A long silence answered her. "I had a little attack of angina. Nothing serious, but I went into the emergency room just to let them poke at me and make some money off my insurance company."

"Angina? A heart attack?" Her own heart clenched with fear. Would she come home to find Samuel the way she'd found her grandfather?

"Relax. It's nothing. I'm not going to die on you any time soon. I promise. Now tell me all about what my grandson's done. What do you mean about him trying to *save* the ranch?"

Hannah swallowed hard. She was being selfish, letting her own feelings, her own comfort, get in the way of helping her friend. Samuel wanted to get to know his grandson, and he didn't have all the time in the world to do it. He needed her help.

She told Samuel about the mortgage and Clayton's determination to pay it off, as well as his problems with the drought. She left out the part about Clayton's putting her in the same category. That still smarted too much to talk about.

"My detective said his mother had taken out a mortgage several years ago," Samuel replied. "But I didn't realize he was having problems paying it off."

"Don't worry," she reassured him, terrified he'd have another attack. "He has your strength of character. He'll manage just fine."

"I know that. I've never had the least doubt that my grandson could handle things. But it's too bad you won't be able to stay and talk to him and—" he sighed wistfully "—convince him I'm not such a bad guy after all."

He was trying to manipulate her. She knew that. She wasn't going to let him do it. Yet she couldn't seem to say the words necessary to refuse him.

"It's my fault my grandson's in this financial mess. I'd sure appreciate it if you could find out some of the details."

"You mean snoop? I couldn't do that!"

"Of course you couldn't. But you already told me you did some work on cleaning up his accounting system. I'd like to know if there's any way I can help...undo some of the problems I've caused."

"You could find him a new housekeeper," she muttered.

"Hannah, please? One more day."

"All right. One more day," she promised. "I'll give it one more day. Then I'm coming home, and I'll...I'll send him faxes about everything over the modem I just hooked up for him." Not that Clayton would know how to set his computer to receive a fax or how to access it to read it afterward.

"Thank you, Hannah. I can't tell you how much this means to me."

Hannah hung up the phone and stared at it for a long moment. The gratitude in Samuel's voice made her sacrifice bearable even though the way Clayton had lumped her with drought and low cattle prices still rankled.

But as she thought about the rest of their conversation, about the way he'd twirled his hat and refused to meet her gaze, she suddenly wondered if Clayton was really as confident as he seemed. If he was so positive he was totally in control of everything, why did he feel it necessary to talk to a man he'd never met, a man he thought was dead?

Her own grandfather had drilled into her head over and over that everybody had insecurities, but she'd always believed she had a corner on the market.

Was it possible Clayton had a few of his own? Was it possible even someone who could dance and run a ranch was not invulnerable?

This was something Hannah needed to think about.

Chapter Nine

"**I** can't fix it," Clayton finally admitted, shaking his head at the pear burner lying lifeless on his work bench. The machine had worked only intermittently over the past three days, slowing their progress and generally being a major pain. "We'll have to get a new part," he concluded.

"I was afraid of that," Dub said. "If you want to call Hank's Hardware before he closes, he'll leave it in a box out back, and I'll go pick it up after dinner."

"Good idea. We need to get this working first thing in the morning. We've lost enough time already. Well, guess we might as well wash up and call it a day." Clayton picked up his hat, glad to escape the confines of the workshop where he and Dub had been laboring over the broken burner for the better part of an hour.

As they rounded the corner and the house came into view, Clayton noticed that the other four hands had congregated around the porch. Even from a couple of hundred feet, he could see Hannah's shiny curls in the middle of the group. She lifted her head, looking at either Bear or Cruiser—he couldn't be sure which—and laughed. The carefree, happy sound danced across the evening air, and a sharp pang that couldn't possibly be jealousy, but certainly felt like it, darted through Clayton's chest.

Over the past few days she'd become more relaxed, especially around the hands. They treated her somewhere between the way they'd treat the Queen and their little sister.

She'd even lost some of her nervousness around him. But the focus of their discussions still centered on his grandfather. Which was probably just as well. When they did lapse into ordinary conversation, he had a tendency to forget himself and open up to her, tell her far more personal things than he intended. She, in turn, shared far more personal things than he wanted to hear—except a part of him did want to hear them, did want to know more of the enigma that was Hannah.

He had to constantly remind himself to keep his hands and his emotions off her.

"What's going on?" he asked. "What's everybody doing out there? What's Hannah doing?"

"I don't know, Boss," Dub drawled, "but I don't reckon there's any reason to get excited."

"I'm not excited. It's just that I never know what Hannah's going to do next."

"Aw, she's okay. You gotta admit, lunch wasn't so bad."

"Not as bad as usual."

"Any idea what it was?"

"I recognized some pieces of chicken. But it's hard to say for sure."

"She sure comes up with some funny stuff."

"That she does. I ordered another gallon of picante sauce."

"They brought Barney up for her to feed!" Dub exclaimed in delight as the calf's hindquarters appeared between Mugger and Bob.

"Why would they do that?" Even as he asked the question, Clayton got his answer. Hannah lifted her face to look at him, and she was beautiful. Her eyes, cheeks, teeth, hair—everything about her was shining and luminous.

Good grief. *Madonna and calf.*

He walked closer, and the cowboys moved aside to give him a spot.

She sat on the porch on a dining-room chair holding the oversize bottle in both hands while the calf—Clayton didn't know when he had acquired the name of Barney—sucked greedily and gazed up at her with adoring eyes.

"He likes me," she said.

No one could deny that Hannah's food was inedible or that her words sometimes fell all over themselves the way she fell over her feet while dancing. She got stuck under his desk and had fantasies about using his computer. She couldn't seem to do anything right...except thoroughly enchant every man and, apparently, every animal, she came into contact with.

From the first, she'd had his rough cowhands treating her like a fairy-tale princess. And, if Clayton were honest with himself, she'd bewitched him, too. It was the only explanation of why he hadn't given her her walking papers after that first awful lunch, of why he'd practically *insisted* she stay!

Clayton sat down on the edge of the porch and stroked the calf's sleek hair. "Of course he likes you."

Hannah looked at him, her cheeks flooding with color followed immediately by a dip of the head and her hair falling forward. But then to his surprise, she lifted her head and gave him a timid smile. "He's kind of like a big dog," she said. "I never had a dog." She hesitated as if she'd drained her conversational resources, then added hurriedly, "Did you?"

Amazing. Hannah was initiating a dialogue with him about something other than their grandfathers.

"Sure," he said. "Lots of them. I took in every stray that wandered up. Why didn't you have a dog?"

"They shed. On Mother's furniture."

"My sister's dog just had puppies," Bear interjected, and Clayton felt an irrational, childish urge to shove his fist down the man's throat for intruding between Hannah and him. "Them little bitty ones with the long hair. I could get you one."

"What are we having for dinner?" Clayton asked in an attempt to change the subject. It was the first thing that came to mind, though he wasn't really sure he wanted to know. It might be better to face it all at once than to have to anticipate it.

"Oh, dear! I forgot the roast!" She turned the bottle over to Bob and darted into the house, presumably to attempt a rescue of the dinner predestined to doom. The screen door slammed behind her.

Clayton watched her go and shook his head to clear the fog.

First he'd wondered if she were psychic. Now he

thought of her as enchanting and bewitching, which was certainly possible. She was messing up his mind in a major way—at a time when he needed to focus every ounce of his energy and thoughts on business, on the ranch. He couldn't let anything or anybody interfere right now.

Especially not someone who'd soon be gone from his life.

Hannah chewed her first bite of the roast. Not too bad, she thought. A little dry, and the outside was kind of hard, but it was edible, and the potatoes were soft on all sides.

Surreptitiously she watched the others as they poured on the picante sauce, cut their meat and lifted it to their mouths. All eyes were focused on their plates.

Then Dub looked up and smiled. Embarrassed at being caught watching, Hannah averted her eyes, but her heart was racing. Did that mean he *approved of* her roast? Did that mean she had finally done it right?

She heard the sound of a chair being scooted back, then clapping. She looked up to see the others slide their chairs out. Everyone began to applaud… everyone except Clayton. Everyone except the man whose approval she wanted in spite of knowing the foolishness and self-destruction of such a need.

Then Clayton rose, too, a sheepish grin on his face as if he were slightly embarrassed at the display. His gaze met hers, and she thought she might explode with happiness.

Bear took her elbow. "Stand up and take a bow. You done good."

Blushing furiously, Hannah rose. "Thank you." She sat back down, and the men followed suit.

Amazing, she thought as everyone began to talk, discussing the day's events, asking about her day. She'd been the center of attention, and she hadn't wanted to drop through a crack in the floor. In fact, she'd kind of enjoyed it. Now she was having a conversation with people she barely knew, and she wasn't even perspiring.

"I made something special for dessert," she blurted, heady with her recent successes—cooking and social.

"All *right!*"

"I'll be sure and save some room."

"I can't wait," Clayton said, his voice soft amid the raucous tones of the cowhands, but his words were the ones she heard the clearest. His words were the ones that echoed over and over in her head. She had finally succeeded at something that counted with Clayton.

After everyone had finished the main course, Hannah, still riding in a golden haze of happiness, carried the dirty dishes to the kitchen.

Taking out a skillet, she carefully measured brown sugar and butter, then cut up six bananas. While the sauce cooked, she scooped ice cream into seven bowls, complimenting herself on her organization. She'd been surprised at the simplicity of the recipe for bananas Foster, a dish that always impressed everyone, including her.

While the brandy heated, she took the ice cream into the dining room and set it on the sideboard.

"Chocolate sundaes?" Mugger guessed.

"No. Better."

"Better than chocolate sundaes? Offhand I can't think of anything better unless it's chocolate sundaes with nuts."

Hannah went back into the kitchen and, holding her breath that it wouldn't explode in her face, lit the brandy. Successfully. And poured it over the banana mixture.

Holding her flaming concoction in front of her, Hannah proudly pushed through the kitchen door into the dining room.

Clayton's eyes widened. "Omigod!" He shot out of his chair and charged toward her.

Hannah gasped and stumbled backward into the kitchen just as he reached her and grabbed her pan. She struggled to hold on, but the sauce splashed onto the floor.

"The kitchen's on fire!" Cruiser raced in and began stomping on the bananas.

Fighting back her tears, Hannah released the skillet to Clayton. Her surprise was ruined. Her evening of glory was ruined...by the man she'd been working so hard to please.

"What'd you do that for?" Bear demanded as they all crowded through the kitchen door.

"I didn't mean—" Hannah began, but Clayton interrupted her.

"It was on fire!" he protested.

Bear, looking very much like his namesake, stood glaring at Clayton.

He was talking to *Clayton*, not to her...blaming Clayton, not her. In that moment her heart went out to the tall, confident, self-assured cowboy. Being in trouble was no fun. She knew that all too well.

"It's okay," she said, but no one seemed to hear her.

"It was one of them fancy desserts," Bob said. "Wudn't nothing burning but the liquor in the pan 'til you sloshed it out on the floor. You blew it, man."

"Big time," Mugger added.

Clayton ducked his head and drew a hand across his forehead, then looked up at her with dismay. "Yes, I did. I'm sorry, Hannah."

Cruiser appeared with a dustpan and began to scoop up the glop on the floor...the glop that, a few minutes ago, had been her special dessert, her claim to fame.

"It's okay," Hannah repeated.

It wasn't, of course.

"No, it's not," he said, as if reading her mind.

She snatched a sponge off the counter and bent to help Cruiser.

Clayton squatted beside her. "Hannah, please talk to me."

Oh, right! He humiliated her then expected her to do something she had trouble with under the best of circumstances—talk.

"I can get this," Cruiser said. "You go on with the boss."

Clayton stood, taking Hannah's arm and urging her up with him. "Let's go out on the porch and get some fresh air."

Dub laid a consoling hand on her back. "Sure looked good before it hit the floor. Think you could make us some more tomorrow night?"

Hannah gave Dub a smile she hoped was reassuring, though she didn't plan to be there tomorrow night.

"The boss didn't mean any harm," Dub went on. "He's been a little edgy here lately."

"Thank you, Dub. I can make my own apologies." Clayton definitely sounded a little edgy.

Hannah wanted to stay in the kitchen. She didn't want to go outside with Clayton. She felt drained and exhausted, incapable of discussing what had just happened, especially with Clayton.

But if he felt half as bad after his blunder as she always did after hers, he might need some comfort. Not that he didn't deserve to feel bad. She could sympathize, but she was still upset with what he'd done...why he'd done it.

She followed him outside, sat on the edge of the porch next to him and stared into the night, unsure what to say.

The evening shadows were kind to the desolate land. The mesquite trees and prickly pear had changed to intriguing, artistic silhouettes. Stars twinkled overhead in the endless velvet sky. A coyote howled in the distance, adding a poignant element to the scene.

"Hannah, I can't begin to tell you how sorry I am. I was one hundred percent wrong." His words brought her back to the situation at hand, the one she didn't want to be brought back to.

"It's all right." She leaned forward, wrapping her arms around her knees.

"Damn it, stop saying that! It's not all right, and we both know it. I was way out of line. You served us a...uh...a delicious dinner and you made a wonderful dessert, and I spoiled it."

"You didn't think I could do it," she accused. "You didn't trust me."

"I overreacted. My only excuse is that I've had a lot on my mind lately, and you've got to admit, you've had a few mishaps."

She had no answer to that. She could have told him she didn't have mishaps with computers, but she saw no point in trying to defend herself. The bananas Foster hadn't been a mishap—until Clayton turned it into one.

"Everybody makes mistakes," Clayton continued. "You've made a couple, and I just made a giant one, big enough to compensate for all of yours, to even the score." He reached for her hand, drawing it away from her knees. But not from her skirt. The fabric stuck, bound by the sticky sauce from her efforts to help clean up the mess on the floor.

Clayton freed the material, then took her hand.

She looked at him and smiled in spite of herself. "You may be stuck with my hand forever. Literally."

He returned her smile. "Then you'll have to forgive me. You can't continue to ignore me if you're permanently attached to me."

She shrugged. She hadn't gotten over the pain of what he'd done, but his words and his touch had a soothing effect.

A wisp of breeze brought the scents of horses, dust and leather to her. The ranch scents belonged to Clayton...as he belonged to the ranch. Sitting outside like this, she could feel the strength and depth of his attachment to this place, his determination to hold on to it.

He lifted one of his hands from hers—the one on top, the one that wasn't stuck—and brushed her curls away from her face.

"You should wear your hair back," he said softly,

"so people can see your face. You have such pretty eyes—" he trailed a finger around one of her eyes, leaving electric tingles in its wake "—and cheek- bones—" and along her cheek "—and lips." His fin- ger traced her bottom lip softly then slid away. His face moved closer to her, his eyes half-closed.

He was going to kiss her again! What had she done before? How had she held her mouth? What—

His lips touched hers, and all doubts vanished as they molded together perfectly.

He slid his arms around her, and she felt her arms slipping around him as if of their own volition. It was amazing how everything seemed to work right when Clayton kissed her.

And then she stopped thinking about it and surren- dered to the softness of his lips, the hardness of his body against hers...to pure sensation.

At the sound of a crash, Hannah sprang away and looked around fearfully. How could kissing Clayton cause a crash?

"Sorry, boss," Dub mumbled, catching the screen door as it swung back from the wall. "Bob pushed me."

"You wouldn't get out of my way," Bob protested.

"I didn't want you to come out here and inter- rupt."

"Looks like we did anyway."

"It's okay, fellows," Clayton said. "We were just going in."

"Going in? Oh, inside. Right. Sure. Okay. We're leaving." Dub was starting to sound like her. "Gotta get to bed. Get an early start." The men swarmed out the door and off the porch, calling their good-nights as they headed toward the bunkhouse.

She watched them go, glad they were gone and wishing they were still there. Now she was alone with Clayton.

On the other hand, now she was alone with Clayton.

That was wonderful, exciting.

That was frightening.

She didn't have a clue what to do next.

Clayton rose beside her, his breath warm on her neck, and she noted that he was breathing fast also, just the way she was.

"Dub sounded funny," she observed, searching for anything to say that didn't center around what she was thinking...whether Clayton would kiss her again.

"They thought we wanted them to leave so we could go upstairs together."

Go upstairs together? It took her a few seconds for the import to register. "You mean, upstairs to...uh... your room. To, uh..."

"To make love," he finished for her, his low tones flowing over her in an almost palpable caress.

She swallowed hard, definitely unable to look at him now.

That was, she supposed, what followed a kiss like the one they'd just shared. Wasn't it? She had no idea of the proper protocol.

"Are we?" she asked, her voice barely above a whisper. "Going upstairs?"

"Do you want to?"

Every cell in her body wanted to, with the exception of her brain cells, which, though locked away in a back room, were protesting loudly.

Clayton's big, callused hand cupped her chin gently

and turned her to face him. To her surprise, Clayton looked as confused as she felt.

"Hannah, you're so beautiful and so—" He took his hand from her chin and dragged his fingers through his hair. "It's like you're from another planet." He shook his head. "You came in and turned everything upside down, including me. I have no idea what to do with you."

That probably meant they weren't going to make love, Hannah decided.

Which was a good thing because she'd have figured out some way to ruin it. Fall off the bed.... Discover she had her underwear on inside out....

She could only cringe at the thought of how her abysmal lack of coordination might affect that sort of activity.

It was definitely a good thing they weren't going to make love.

Her body could just get over its disappointment.

"Are you ready to go in?" he asked.

She nodded.

Clayton stepped out of the shower and dried himself briskly. So much for that old wives' tale about a cold shower cooling a guy's desire.

The really stupid part was, Hannah probably would have come up here with him. He could be holding her slim body next to his right now instead of trying to forget how that body felt in his arms, how eagerly she returned his kiss.

But he just couldn't do it. She was too innocent, too trusting. She wasn't the type to indulge in an evening's entertainment and forget about it, nor was she the type he could afford to become involved with. His first impression of her had been right—fragile and unequipped to deal with the harsh realities of life. Maybe she wasn't as much of a space cadet as he'd first thought, but she sure wasn't a stable, both-feet-planted-on-the-earth type either.

She was uniquely Hannah. A woman who'd already disrupted his life far too much and had the potential for even more disruption.

This was tough country where only the rugged could survive. Lizards and coyotes, stunted mesquite trees, long-horned and Brahman cattle, tumbleweeds, prickly pear cacti, and cowboys like him thrived on it. Delicate flowers with sweet scents and velvet-soft blossoms like Hannah...like his mother, his grandmother and grandfather...they wilted and died or ran for their lives.

Clayton hung up his towel and walked into his bedroom. Clean underwear, blue jeans and shirts were stacked on his bed.

If he overlooked the facts that she'd started the laundry three days ago, that she hadn't hung up any of the clothes and that the bed was unmade, he could be pleased that Hannah was getting the hang of this housekeeping thing after all. She'd cooked a dinner that he could eat without choking, and she'd managed the laundry even if it had taken a bit longer than normal. That was an improvement.

He put away his shorts and socks then got hangers from the closet and lifted a pair of blue jeans. New, stiff blue jeans. He didn't own any new blue jeans.

He picked up the next pair. They were new, too.

All the shirts and blue jeans were new. Had Hannah given him the wrong laundry? He didn't remember any of the guys having new clothes, but that was the only explanation. He might have been willing to believe Hannah could make *new* clothes *old*. She was aging him rapidly. But she couldn't possibly turn old into new.

He slipped on a pair of old jeans, went down the hall to her room and knocked.

She opened the door a crack and peered out at him.

"Hannah, can you come to my room a minute?"

Her gaze darted downward then back up to his face, her dark, luminous eyes widening in surprise, fear and a little anticipation. "Oh!" was all she said.

He suddenly realized what she must be thinking. He'd come to her room wearing only blue jeans, no shirt or shoes, and asked her to go to his room.

"I, uh, need to show you something." That came out all wrong. "Ask you something." Good grief! She had him doing it now, tripping over his own tongue! "About the laundry."

"Oh." She opened the door wider, and he saw that she was wearing a fluffy, pale yellow robe that had probably been nice several years ago. It was baggy and worn and covered every inch of her from her chin to her toes, but somehow on Hannah it became the sexiest garment Clayton had ever seen.

She preceded him down the hall to his room, her rounded bottom outlined by the fabric, moving with each step she took, and he wondered if he'd really seen new clothes on his bed. Maybe it was only a hallucination his testosterone had conjured up to give him a reason to lure her down to his room.

He went in behind her, forbidding himself to close the door. "These clothes—" he indicated the piles "—they're not mine."

She lowered her eyes and fiddled with the sash of her robe. "There was an accident," she mumbled.

"An accident?" He had an absurd vision of one of his shirts speeding down the street, running a red light and crashing into a pair of jeans. "What kind of an accident?"

She raised her eyes and took a deep breath. "All the spots came out."

Just when he'd begun to believe she was going to make it after all. "That doesn't explain why the clothes are new."

She had her sash twisted so tight he thought it might tear, rip in two and allow her robe to part, to reveal the rest of the creamy white skin that disappeared behind the open V-neck.

"The spots left holes, and I knew you weren't the trendy type, so I ordered new clothes for you. I put them on my account, and the store delivered them today. I found the sizes on your old ones, but they didn't have some of the brands."

Clayton stared at her in dismay. She'd ruined his clothes and had to buy replacements? She hadn't even managed to get the laundry right?

He would have liked to know how she had turned his spots into holes, but decided not to ask. If he hadn't seen her putting stain remover on them, he'd have considered the possibility that she'd cut out the soiled places.

"Are they wrong?" she asked tentatively. "I can have them returned."

"They're fine. I'm sure they're fine." *Fine?* What was the matter with him? She'd done something else wrong. Somehow she'd ruined the broken-in, comfortable jeans and shirts he loved and replaced them with stiff new ones. Yet instead of chastising her, he was reassuring her.

He tore his gaze from her before he lost control completely and told her how much he'd hated those old clothes and how glad he was to get rid of them. Maybe if he didn't look at her, she wouldn't be able to cast her spell over him.

It didn't matter. The unmade bed sprang into his field of vision, beckoning him, suggesting how she might look amid those rumpled covers. Damn, he wished she'd made it up the way Mrs. Grogan used to do, with the sheets stretched tight, covers all in place, pillows plumped...neat, tidy and uninviting.

"I noticed you haven't been making my bed," he blurted out.

She seemed mystified by his accusation. "Make the bed? You mean, every morning?"

Knowing her, she might think he meant that literally—take a hammer and nails and make a bed. "Straighten the covers. Fluff the pillows. Put the spread on top."

She nodded slowly, uncomprehendingly, then shook her head. "Wash the sheets every morning?"

Considering the outcome of her doing his laundry, he didn't think she could afford to wash the sheets every day. "No. Wash the sheets once a week. Make the bed every day," he said patiently.

"But—you sleep in that bed."

"That's true. But only at night. It can sit here made up the whole day while I'm working."

"You should air it during the day so it'll be fresh at night. Why would you want to cover up the sheets after you've slept in them? That doesn't sound very hygienic. Anyway, what benefit do you derive from it being made while you're gone? You'll only see it at night before you unmake it.''

She was doing it again. Talking complete nonsense and making it sound reasonable.

She stood beside his bed, inches away from him, nervously twisting the other end of that sash, looking at him tentatively and smelling faintly of roses. She was fragile and insecure and incompetent and as wrong for him as it was possible for any woman to be. And he wanted to pull her into his arms and sink into the unmade bed with her, hold her all night and all day.

Which would greatly interfere with running the ranch.

"Tomorrow, would you please make my bed and clean the house?" He threw the words into the space between them, needing to push her away before it was too late.

"Clean the house?" she repeated.

"Dust, vacuum, mop the floors, clean the bathrooms.''

"Clean the house." Even though her words were a statement and not a question this time, they didn't sound like agreement. He halfway expected her to argue with him about the benefits of a clean house, and right now he wasn't sure he'd be able to defend his position. Right now all he could think about was her nearness, her eyes, her lips, the way she'd kissed him out on the porch.

"Tomorrow," she said, and just before she dropped her eyes, Clayton thought their liquid depths had solidified to marble. Must be shadows from the harsh electric lighting.

Fortunately, and to his regret, she slipped past him and left the room.

He recalled again his first impression of her as a spiderweb wet with dew glistening in the sunlight. She was every bit as intricate, intriguing and susceptible to devastation as that image.

Clayton tossed and turned in his unmade bed for over an hour before he remembered the pear burner. He had never called Hank's Hardware to arrange to have the part left outside for Dub to pick up. He had forgotten.

From the time he'd walked up to the house and seen Hannah feeding that calf, he'd thought of nothing but her.

Hannah—his fascination with Hannah—wasn't just messing up his mind. It was messing up his life. He would lose valuable daylight hours tomorrow because of this lapse.

He couldn't keep Hannah around. He had to let her go. It was the only sensible thing to do. For both their sakes. Before she distracted him so completely he lost all touch with his responsibilities and before the ranch shattered her into beautiful, shiny pieces just the way the crystal vase had shattered.

With that resolution, he settled down to spend the rest of the night tossing and turning.

Chapter Ten

The following evening Clayton trailed behind Hannah and the guys as they trekked upstairs to his office...to his computer. He wasn't sure how he went from a restless night spent rehearsing ways of firing Hannah to the next day giving her permission to teach the boys to play computer games.

When they'd all gathered at the corral first thing that morning to discuss the day's tasks, Clayton had asked Dub to go for the pear burner part after breakfast.

"Will do," Dub said, swinging into the saddle. "And while I'm there, Hannah told us if we got some computer games and if you said it was all right to use your computer, she'd teach us how to play them. There's a big electronics store just down from Hank's. Be right on my way."

"You think Hannah can teach you to play computer games?" Clayton asked incredulously.

"She's made up some games herself," Bob protested. "She gave us the names so we could try to find them."

"Look, guys, I realize that Hannah is...Hannah is..." He was at a loss for words to describe Hannah. Maybe because too many words came to mind all at once. Hannah was too complex to describe at five o'clock in the morning after a sleepless night.

"Our friend," Bear finished for him. "Hannah's our friend."

"And she wants to teach us her games, so we want to learn them," Mugger added.

Clayton took off his hat and ran a hand through his hair as he blew out a long breath. Had it really only been last week when his life had been so simple, his only problems the lack of a cook, a major drought, low cattle prices and a mortgage hanging over his head?

"I understand that Hannah is your friend, but have any of you stopped to consider how farfetched this whole idea is? Hannah can't even make a decent meal or do laundry. How could she possibly play, much less write, computer programs?"

"You can't run a computer, but you know ranching backwards and forwards," Dub persisted. "I reckon God give us all different talents. We'd sure be up a creek if He didn't."

The men all looked at him silently, expectantly. He wanted to say *no*. He feared for the life of his computer with the six of them experimenting with things they knew nothing about. But mostly, he knew how upset Hannah got when things didn't turn out right, and he didn't want her to be embarrassed in front of her new friends.

"Come on, boss," Dub said, "Hannah wants to

impress us. Let her do it. She feels awful when her meals don't turn out so good. This'll give her a chance to shine."

And heaven only knew what she could do with a computer, what kind of chaos she could create.

"Look, if Hannah really does write computer games, what's she doing working as a housekeeper out here?"

"I dunno. Maybe those computer games don't pay so good."

"For crying out loud! Look there, boss," Cruiser exclaimed, pointing to a dark object meandering slowly toward a cluster of mesquite trees. "Is that what I think it is?"

"Yeah, it's a porcupine. He's been hanging around the last few days. I'm not sure what he's doing down here, but he'll head on back to greener territory soon." Just as Hannah would. And should. The sooner the better.

"All right. Get your computer games." Clayton urged his horse forward, into the morning.

After Hannah humiliated herself at the computer, she'd probably turn tail and run back home, the way that out-of-place porcupine would be doing any day now.

When Dub had returned just before lunch with two computer games, Hannah had excitedly identified one called *Dragon Ride to the Stars* as hers. It did sound like something she'd think of—a fairy-tale creature heading for the stars. But he'd peeked at the label. Her name wasn't on there.

He'd tried to talk her out of this game session. He'd even given her several excuses to go to bed early and save herself from the impending embarrassment, but after dinner she'd been eager to get started.

He followed the guys into his office and found her already seated in front of his computer, tossing around buzz words in an excited voice. Whatever happened next, he'd certainly never seen her that enthusiastic about housework.

Hannah fought the slight trembling that wanted to possess her fingers as she put *Dragon Ride to the Stars* through its paces. Clayton leaned against the wall, arms folded across his chest, glowering as if he expected her to pour bleach on his computer and eat holes in the screen or blow the whole thing up.

She'd been surprised that he'd agreed to let her use his computer at all, and she knew the only reason he'd come along was to guard it.

But this was one thing she wasn't going to mess up.

She set the game for two players. "Okay, who's going to go first?"

"Dub is!" The other men shoved a stumbling, blushing Dub forward.

"I'm not real good at things like this," he mumbled, taking the folding chair Clayton offered him.

"It's easy. I'll show you," Hannah reassured him.

An hour later everyone had taken a turn except Clayton. He hadn't moved, hadn't joined in the cheering, the laughter or the good-natured ribbing. If not for his eyes, which she could feel following her every move, Hannah would have thought he'd gone to sleep or turned to stone.

"Okay, boss," Dub said, "your turn."

For a long moment Clayton didn't move, then he slowly unfolded his arms. "I'll pass."

How unfair! She had to meet him every day in his field of expertise, but he refused to enter hers.

You can't do that! she thought, then realized with shock and dismay that she'd spoken the words aloud.

"Yeah, boss," Bear urged. "Get on over here. It's fun. I reckon we'll have to get one of these things for the bunkhouse. Beats hell...er, heck...out of watching television."

"And next we can all learn to ski that Internet," Mugger added.

Amazed at her own daring, Hannah looked Clayton squarely in the eye, challenging him.

He shrugged, unfolded himself and moseyed over to sit beside her.

Close beside her.

Maybe this wasn't such a good idea after all. His denim-clad thigh pressing against hers flustered her, made her feel as if she were sitting in front of the uncharted territory of a kitchen stove instead of her old friend, a computer.

She restarted the game and ordered herself to narrow her focus, to exclude the mind-numbing, heart-stopping effects of Clayton's body so close to hers, of his familiar scent wrapping around and caressing her....

Cataloging the elements she was trying to ignore wasn't a good way to ignore them.

"Take a practice run," she offered. That would give her a chance to find some composure.

"I don't need to practice. I've been sitting here all evening watching."

He took the controls and began. He had been paying attention and he seemed to have a natural aptitude.

Silence surrounded them, heavy and tense, as if all the guys were holding their breath, waiting.

She'd helped each one of them play, had given them unwarranted chances and pulled back on her own efforts so each game had been close. But some instinct she hadn't known she possessed rose up with Clayton as her opponent. She wanted to win and win big. She wanted to trounce him. She wanted to beat him so badly he'd have to admit she could do something well.

When he handed her the controls, that instinct took over and she began to play.

Clayton had watched all evening in growing astonishment as she deftly maneuvered through the levels of the computer game. Now that astonishment reached epic proportions. She had become a different person...competent, sure of herself, in charge...out for blood.

Being forced to sit beside her, to feel the warmth of her body, was disconcerting enough, but this new aspect threw him for a loop.

He lost.

Big time.

And all his loyal ranch hands cheered for Hannah. They patted her on the back, congratulated her and, laughing and talking, finally left.

Clayton scooted out his folding chair and stood, forcing a smile onto his face.

"That was fun," he lied.

She beamed up at him, once again the shy girl looking for approval, her bloodlust vanished. "Really?"

His tense smile relaxed into a genuine one. Okay, she was entitled to win once in a while. He'd just gotten a taste of what it was like to fail...and to fail in front of a crowd. No wonder she was so sensitive about that sort of thing.

"Really. You're very good."

She blushed, but this was a happy blush, not painful as most of her blushes were. "Only because I created the game."

He didn't know what to say to that. He couldn't accuse her of lying.

Maybe she believed what she said. After all, she'd come there with the delusion that she could keep house and cook. Maybe so many years of failure at so many things had led her to think she could do things she really couldn't.

"You don't believe me, do you?" Her voice and expression were guileless with a touch of pain.

He cleared his throat and shifted from one foot to the other. "If you wrote it, why isn't your name on the label?"

She rose from the chair, her chin lifted slightly, her posture a study in righteous indignation. "The company I work for takes copyright in their name. Just because I can't sing or dance or cook doesn't mean there aren't other things I can do. You can't use a computer, so that makes us even."

Head high, she strode from the room.

Clayton started after her. "Hannah, I didn't mean—"

She slammed the door to her bedroom behind her, leaving Clayton standing in the hallway. Exasperated, he raked a hand through his hair and stared at the floor. She certainly was touchy. And after she'd just walloped him good at *her* game.

It was possible, he thought. Computer nerds were

notorious for not being able to function in the real world.

But Hannah didn't look like a computer nerd was supposed to look. She was soft and smooth and slim and rounded and felt wonderful in his arms.

She didn't kiss like a computer nerd, either.

Not that he had any idea how a computer nerd kissed.

He lifted a hand to knock and apologize, then stopped before he made contact with the wood.

If he knocked and she opened the door and gazed up at him and made him go all mushy inside and he apologized and told her it didn't matter if she wrote computer programs or cooked awful meals or ruined his shirts, that all that mattered was holding her and touching her...

That was no good.

So what if she wrote computer programs? She was still Hannah, delicate, desirable Hannah. She still stole his thoughts from his responsibilities, from taking care of the ranch. She was still as out of place here as that pitiful, lost porcupine.

He dropped his hand, then shoved it into his pocket just to be sure it wouldn't try anything foolish—like reaching for the knob and opening that door.

He'd better get to bed. Tomorrow, like every other day, would be a rough one.

As to what he was going to do about the enigma that was Hannah, he had no idea. Maybe she was so upset with him, she'd leave of her own volition and he wouldn't have to do anything. That would be the best possible solution.

He knew that.

So why did that solution make his chest feel empty and achy?

Chapter Eleven

Hannah consulted her cookbook only sporadically while cooking breakfast the next morning. What difference did it make? The hollandaise sauce was doomed to lumps whatever she did or didn't do.

She'd never be able to cook, wash and clean to Clayton's satisfaction and nothing else mattered to him. She'd proven her competence with a computer, and he still thought she was a failure, such a complete failure it wasn't conceivable that she could have designed her own program.

At least she had a cold cola this morning since she'd included a six-pack in her recent grocery order. She popped the top and took a long swallow.

Somehow the soft drink didn't have its usual effervescent effect.

She dumped new coffee grounds into the basket then noticed she hadn't removed the old ones. Oh, well. They'd drunk coffee made from the old ones yesterday without complaint. Surely something as vile as coffee wouldn't spoil.

She poured in the water then popped another English muffin into the toaster. There was no way she could make it do more than one at a time. When the last one was done, the first would be cold...as cold as Clayton had been to her last night. She wasn't likely to get a standing ovation for this meal.

That had been nice, she reflected, when the cowboys had applauded her culinary efforts.

But it didn't matter. However many things she did right, all Clayton would ever see were the ones she did wrong.

She understood people like him only too well. Her parents hadn't been proud that she'd been valedictorian, that she'd been offered several scholarships from prestigious colleges. All they'd seen were the failures in the things that counted with them, the social activities.

Taking care of this ranch was what counted with Clayton. And no matter how soft his lips were when he kissed her, no matter that his heart pounded as wildly as hers, she was still a failure.

She didn't like the way that made her feel inside—all shriveled and dry like a prune. She enjoyed feeling good, the way she had when she'd told her grandfather about her scholarships, the way she had when the guys had applauded her half-decent dinner.

She dropped an egg into a pan of water. It spread out in little white threads. It didn't look like any poached egg she'd ever eaten, but maybe it would cook back together or something. She added more eggs. That should help. They wouldn't have room to spread out.

This evening she'd tell Clayton the truth and plead Samuel's case. That was the best she could do. The longer she stayed, the less credible she became.

Then she'd go back home where she could feel comfortable and safe again, where she could forget she'd ever run into Clayton and his tempting, hurtful lips.

She checked the eggs. Some of them were sticking together, but there were still lots of white pieces and a few fragments of yolks floating around.

Oh, well. Things couldn't get any worse.

As the men came in and took their seats, Hannah stared down at the eggs Benedict on her plate and found herself hoping that the food would be good. In spite of all her rationale, she still wanted Dub, Bear, Cruiser, Mugger, Bob and especially Clayton to be pleased with her efforts.

Though the hands were their usual selves, laughing and joking, Clayton sat at the end of the table, his gaze glued to his plate, refusing to look at her. Indignation swelled inside her. What right did he have to measure her worth by her housekeeping skills?

"Got a good chance of rain today," Dub said, pouring on the picante sauce.

"Really?" Hannah asked. "How do you know? The sun's out, and the weather report didn't say anything about rain."

"I can feel it in my bones. 'Specially my left leg, the one that got broke when a stallion threw me a few years back."

"My granddad used to say he could tell by his old war wound," Hannah said.

"Which war was your granddaddy in?" Bear asked.

"Oh, he wasn't in a war. But every time I mentioned that, he said I shouldn't be so logical."

To her delight, everyone laughed. Even Clayton lifted his gaze from his plate and, as if reluctantly, a grin tilted the corners of his mouth upward. Slowly the grin widened and sunburst crinkles broke out around his eyes. The others stopped laughing, and the conversation moved on to other things and still he stared at her, his eyes holding hers as surely as his arms had held her when he'd kissed her on the front porch aeons ago.

What could be going through his mind? The last she'd known, he'd refused to believe she was competent enough to write a computer game.

Clayton hadn't meant to look at Hannah. He didn't want to gaze into those eyes that were translucent windows to her emotions. He didn't want to know what she was feeling. But her comment had surprised him. She was losing her shyness rapidly.

Now he feared he could never *stop* looking at her. Just the sight of her at the end of the table made him feel inexplicably happy.

There was absolutely no reason for it. Her latest concoction was right up there with the worst. Some kind of chunky sauce over a soggy muffin, crunchy Canadian bacon and semiscrambled, wet eggs. The coffee was, far and away, the worst he'd ever had. If they weren't in the middle of dry, barren brush country, he'd swear she used swamp water to make it.

And still, something glowed inside him at the sight of her. He wanted to gaze into her eyes the rest of the day. If he looked away, he'd see the real world.

It was waiting just outside Hannah's eyes, waiting to steal that irrational glow she gave him.

"Were any of you around when Clayton's grandfather was here?" Hannah asked.

Clayton blinked. The woman sure knew how to destroy a mood. What was it with her and his grandfather?

Silence fell over the table. The jar of picante sauce made another round.

Thank goodness the grandfather topic had fallen flat.

"I grew up around these parts," Bear said abruptly. "Used to come over here sometimes with my daddy. I wudn't but about ten years old when Sam Sinclair left, but I remember him."

"What was he like?"

Bear stroked his beard and shot Clayton an uncomfortable look. Clayton supposed his antagonism toward his grandfather was no secret. Though it wasn't exactly a forbidden topic, surely Bear would know he didn't want it discussed.

"A lot like the boss," Bear said. So much for counting on the man's tact. Obviously Hannah had Bear in her spell, too. "Except he used to give me candy. The boss sure don't do that!"

Everyone laughed, and Clayton had no choice but to join them, though his laughter sounded hollow to him.

"Why did he leave?" Hannah asked. Clayton had already told her the answer to that question. Why was she bringing it up again?

"His only boy, Clayton's daddy, got killed when a horse threw him. Then his wife, Clayton's grandma,

had a heart attack and died. That old man loved both
of them so much, it plumb broke his heart."

He was weak, Clayton wanted to say. *He left because he wasn't strong enough to deal with the life
out here in this part of Texas that demanded so much
of those who loved it.*

He'd figured that out twenty years ago. He knew it
was true. He'd never doubted it.

So why today, all of a sudden, coming out of nowhere, did he find a wisp of sympathy for the man
who'd turned his and his mother's life upside down?
Obviously Hannah must have done something to his
mind for him to be able to consider, for even an instant, such devastating love and devotion touching.

"I reckon he just went off, crawled into a hole
somewhere and died of grief," Bear continued. "I
'spect we'll come across his bones out there one
day."

"Bear! That's enough." Clayton watched Hannah
carefully to see if the grisly picture Bear had painted
would upset her fragile sensibilities.

To his surprise, she showed no reaction.

"Maybe he didn't die," Hannah said enthusiasti-
cally. "Maybe he had a nervous breakdown from the
pain of losing everybody he loved, and he went away
to recover and didn't see any reason to come back
since he didn't know he had a grandson."

No wonder she didn't react to Bear's fantasy. She
had her own fantasy going.

"Yeah," Bob said. "Maybe he got that *amnesia*
because he couldn't stand to remember losing his wife
and his son. Maybe he'll get his memory back and
come home one day."

"That could happen," Mugger agreed. "I saw it in

a movie. The guy went off and got married and had a whole other family, then one day he got hit on the head and remembered who he was and went home.''

''I saw that movie,'' Dub said. ''He came back just as his first grandson was being born. Of course, in this case, it'd have to be his great-grandson.''

Good grief. Hannah was contagious. She had his hardened cowboys out in lala land.

She looked directly at him then. ''That would be really nice, wouldn't it? Having somebody show up you thought was dead, somebody who loved you even though he'd never met you but because you shared the same heritage.''

Her dark eyes pulled him, and he realized he was nodding, was thinking how nice it would be. She had him reverting to the boy who'd waited for his grandfather to come home and rescue his mother and him, the grandfather who never came.

''No!'' he exclaimed, bolting up from his chair and tossing his napkin onto the table. ''You people are talking nonsense. The heat's fried your brains. Come on. We've got work to do.''

Without thinking, he chugged down the rest of his coffee and instantly regretted it. He'd better take a pack of gum with him and try to get rid of that taste.

''Hannah, I'm having a load of hay delivered today. I'll leave you a check to give to the driver.''

Clayton did a quick mental search for any possible ways Hannah could mess up that task. He couldn't think of any...but she had shown herself to be creative.

He went upstairs to his office, wrote out the check and came back down. The table was clear, and Hannah was nowhere to be seen.

He pushed open the kitchen door to see her standing in the midst of the chaos, looking frazzled and confused.

"Hannah, have you ever considered doing something besides housework? Maybe you'd be happier with something a little simpler."

She sighed and smiled wistfully. "Oh, yes. I would definitely be happier doing something less complex and stressful than this." She waved a hand vaguely about the room.

That cinched it, then. She didn't want to be there. He'd be doing both of them a favor to let her go.

So do it, he ordered himself. *Say the words. Make both of you happy.*

But he found himself as speechless as Hannah had been when she'd first arrived.

"Tonight," she said, "we need to talk."

"Yes. We do." She didn't sound any happier about the prospect than he did.

A picture of coming back at the end of a long, hard day to a house without Hannah flashed across his mind. The picture made him sad.

Well, if that wasn't about the dumbest thing he'd come up with yet! Coming back to a ranch house without Hannah meant he could count on coming back to it in the same condition as he left it. No new clothes for old. No soggy noodles or fried porcupines.

He shoved the check into her hand and jammed his hat onto his head. He had to keep the sun from destroying what few brain cells he might have left.

"Tonight," he said as he strode out the door. Odd. He'd never before noticed what a lonely sound the word had.

Hannah folded the check and put it into her skirt pocket then looked around the room. *Something a little simpler.* He was right about that. Would she ever be glad to get back to her computer.

The phone rang, and she went into the living room to answer it, relieved to get away from the dirty dishes, pots and pans for the moment.

"Is Clayton around?" The voice was feminine, young, self-confident and crisp, and cut through Hannah's breast like a knife. It had never occurred to her that Clayton might have a love interest. But why shouldn't he? He was single, good-looking, sexy, and a fantastic kisser. This woman was probably beautiful and graceful and could dance and cook.

"No," she managed to choke out in answer to the woman's question.

"Oh, darn. I wanted to catch him before he went back out after breakfast. Are you the new housekeeper?"

"Yes." *Soon to be the former housekeeper.*

"Oh, well, then it doesn't matter. I'm Lydia, his neighbor. I was calling to tell him that we're going to have to let our housekeeper go, and I thought he might want to hire her. I didn't realize he'd already found someone. If you need anything, even if it's just to talk to another woman after being around those macho cowboys all the time, give me a shout. Our spread's only about ten miles west. What's your name?"

"Hannah." *Our* spread? Did that mean she had a husband?

"I'm sure I'll be meeting you, Hannah, once things slow down. Clayton and I go back a long way. Back to diapers, in fact." She laughed, a rich, easy sound that Hannah envied but decided she didn't have to hate the woman for. If Lydia wasn't planning to see Clayton until things slowed down, they could hardly be romantically involved, could they?

Not that she cared. She was leaving tonight.

"Don't even bother to tell him I called," Lydia said.

"I'm leaving," Hannah blurted out. "He needs your housekeeper. Unless you're letting her go because she can't cook."

"Oh, Marjorie's a terrific cook! We just have to cut back on expenses. This drought's hurt everybody. But why are you leaving so soon?"

How was she supposed to answer that question in twenty-five words or less? "I have another job." It was the truth and didn't require a half-hour explanation.

"Oh, I see. Well, I can't say I blame you. It's a tough life out here. Tell Clayton to call me, then."

Hannah hung up the phone and glared at it.

Tough life. She was getting tired of hearing everybody complain about the *tough life.* They brought a lot of it on themselves, expecting all those hot meals and wanting empty chairs and the beds made every day.

But that wasn't what upset her about the phone call.

Clayton had a chance to get an authentic housekeeper. That made her leaving real. She'd be back home by this time tomorrow. Back in her familiar, safe world.

The nightmare was almost over.

She'd never see Clayton again.

The dream was almost over.

With numb fingers, she lifted the phone to call
Samuel.

He sighed when she told him of her plans. "I understand. I don't suppose you'd consider staying until
this Marjorie gets there?"

"Samuel, you're not hearing me. The longer I stay,
the worse it gets, the more things Clayton finds wrong
with me. I'm probably the worst possible represen-
tative you could have."

"Well, I guess I've done all I can do."

That was an odd comment, Hannah thought. He
hadn't done anything except send her out here to be
humiliated. She let it go. "Me, too," she said. "I've
done all I can do. I'm sorry." *Sorry Clayton will
never know what a wonderful grandfather he has,
sorry I can't seem to please him, and sorry it bothers
me.*

She hung up, and realized she'd failed again. She
hadn't been able to help Samuel anymore than she'd
been able to help her grandfather.

But she had one more slim chance. Tell Clayton
the truth and see what happened.

However, if she expected him to give any credence
to what she had to say, she'd better get on with the
repetitive, boring housework. That seemed to be the
only thing that impressed him.

She'd seen some pork chops in the freezer. If she
stuck them all together with toothpicks, they'd be like
a pork roast, and she could pop them in the oven and
forget them. Pork roast frozen dinners usually had
corn and applesauce or sweet potatoes. Those came
in cans. She could open cans.

Finally lunch was cooking and the kitchen cleaned
up. If she had to clean that room one more time, she'd

surely run from it screaming. The yellow countertop had, she felt certain, lightened several shades from her continual wiping. She took a deep breath and looked around. Now what else had he said?

Dust, vacuum, mop the floors, clean the bathrooms.

She walked through the living room, pausing to check the surfaces of one of the swarm of little tables littering the area. It didn't look too bad. Drawing a finger carefully around the base of a lamp, she noticed the difference. But as long as nobody disturbed the dust's regular dispersion of molecules, it didn't show. Best to let sleeping dust lie.

She'd better go make Clayton's bed, though. For some reason, that seemed to be a hot spot with him.

She climbed the stairs to his room, ignoring the siren call of the computer just across the hall.

What a mess his bed was! Covers every which way, pillows on the floor. If she didn't know better, she'd think...

No. That wasn't possible. She'd have noticed if anyone came to Clayton's room in the middle of the night. Anyway, it was none of her business.

She set about straightening. But every movement of the sheets dispersed Clayton's scent into the air, into her nostrils. She picked up a pillow and held it to her face, closing her eyes and remembering the way his lips had felt when he'd kissed her, the strength in his hands when he'd steadied her the night he tried to teach her to dance, and the gentleness in his touch when he brushed her hair back from her face...the way he made her feel cherished and graceful.

Irritated with herself, she flung the pillow onto the bed. Wasn't she forgetting about the way he'd tackled her and ruined her bananas Foster, possibly the only good thing she'd ever cooked? The way he'd refused to believe she could write computer games? The way he made her feel like a clumsy adolescent?

She yanked the spread up and covered the leather and earth scent that belonged so personally to Clayton. Now, at last, she could see a logical reason for making a bed.

With a great deal of reservation, she walked into the bathroom.

Bad move. She could so easily imagine Clayton standing in the tub with water from the showerhead cascading over his muscled body, glistening in the mat of hairs on his chest. She had a hard enough time forgetting the way his chest had looked when he'd come to her room wearing only his blue jeans.

She turned away and surveyed the small room. Neat and tidy, towels folded and hung over the shower rod. No toiletries sitting out on the vanity. If she could just avoid that tub, cleaning shouldn't be too tough.

Under the sink she found some cleanser, shook some into the stool and scrubbed the sides with the brush. If she let it soak, it would probably work even better. She remembered seeing cleanser in her bathroom after her cleaning lady left.

A few swipes with a washcloth took care of the sink, and all that was left was the tub. Not only did she not want to spend time cleaning the large surface, but she didn't want to become too closely involved with something that conjured up such intimate images of Clayton.

If she turned on the shower and wet it thoroughly, then sprinkled on the cleanser and let it soak, when

Clayton took a shower before dinner and moved his feet around, the work would be done. She sprinkled in a generous amount, closed the curtain and left the room.

Housework was exhausting, time-consuming and unrewarding.

Maybe she could get on the computer for a few minutes, just to relax. She could do a little more work on Clayton's accounts, maybe even reconcile all those bank statements she'd seen lying around. It would be compensation for all the messes she'd made.

In fact, with the modem working, she could get some accounting software from her computer at home that would bring Clayton's operation into the twentieth century. She wouldn't be here to see it, but eventually he'd realize that she hadn't been a total incompetent.

Chapter Twelve

Clayton slid off his horse in disgust. The saddle would have to be cleaned, but he'd had no choice other than to ride to the house. It was too far to walk.

Hannah's catastrophes were definitely contagious. The irrigation line had broken again, and, in the process of repairing it, he'd slipped and fallen backward into the mud. About the only part of him that had escaped the gunky mess was the tip of his nose.

The single good thing so far today was the formation of clouds low on the horizon. Between that and Dub's aching bones, maybe they had a chance for a little rain. Surely he'd run out his string of bad luck by now. He'd been running it pretty hard here lately.

He stood in front of the house and considered his options to resolve this latest problem. He could rinse off at the outside faucet. In this heat, he'd dry quickly.

Or he could go in for a quick shower. He decided he might as well take the extra five minutes to shower.

His decision had absolutely nothing to do with the fact that he'd see Hannah if he went inside. What difference could seeing her one more time make, anyway? She was a delicate flower, an orchid who couldn't survive in the desert, and she'd be going back to her hothouse environment soon. She'd find a job in the city making tea and little sandwiches with no crusts for an elderly lady. Surely her tea would be better than her coffee.

He pulled off his shoes on the porch then hesitated. If the crusty Mrs. Grogan were still here, he'd think nothing of pulling off his jeans and shirt, too, but Hannah would undoubtedly be shocked at the sight of a half-naked, muddy man stalking through the house.

However, the mud was already drying and flaking off. He could imagine his mother's reaction to his walking over her imported rugs and hardwood floors, trickling bits of dirt. The pants and shirt had to come off. He could only hope to sneak in without Hannah seeing him.

Using his fingers, he combed as much of the dried stuff out of his hair as he could, then, clad in nothing but his briefs, stole quietly into the house. No sign of Hannah. She was probably in the kitchen torturing lunch. He could smell something cooking.

He made it upstairs and, keeping an eye on Hannah's door down the hall in case she should suddenly appear, into his bedroom.

To his surprise and delight, the bed was made, in a manner of speaking. At least, it was more orderly than when he'd left it.

The bath smelled of cleanser. Hannah had been busy. She was trying.

He veered his thoughts away from the direction they were taking.

It didn't matter if she was trying. She was causing all sorts of problems. She wasn't suited to this place. It would break her if she didn't get away.

Resolve firmly in place, he stripped off his briefs, turned on the shower and stepped into the tub...then screamed as his feet slid out from under him and he thudded to the floor.

Green, gritty, soapy stuff surrounded him while the shower pummeled him from above. What the hell was going on?

"Clayton, are you hurt?"

He shoved the shower curtain aside to see Hannah in the open doorway.

She turned bright red, gasped and looked away.

"I'm fine," he grated, trying in vain to shield his eyes from the pelting water. "Just wonderful. Hannah, do you know anything about this stuff in my shower?"

"Well, yes. It's cleanser. Why are you taking a shower in the middle of the day? Are you sure you're not hurt? The whole floor shook when you landed."

"Were you anywhere near the irrigation line this morning?"

"No. I've been right here. I don't even know where the irrigation line is. Why?"

"Never mind. Could you, uh, wait in the other room, and I'll be right out."

"Oh, of course. I'll be in your office. I have something to show you."

Her words got him showered and dressed in record time.

He charged across the hall into his office and found

her sitting in the chair with her back to the computer looking excited, smug and timid at the same time. The computer showed a screen he'd never seen before.

"I'm sorry you fell in the tub, but I have some great news for you. I put all your records on the computer and reconciled your bank statements and, look—" She turned to the computer, moved the mouse with one hand, pointed to the screen with the other and began to speak in a foreign language.

"Hannah, I don't understand a word you're saying. What are you talking about? What have you done to my computer?"

She turned back, gazing at him in astonishment and dismay. "I was just trying to show you how you have more money in the bank than you realized, and by doing some simple restructuring and reallocation of assets, you can actually show a small profit this year."

"What?"

"I'll print it all out for you." She moved the mouse around, and the printer sprang to life. She looked at him again. "Clayton, I have a confession. I'm not really a housekeeper."

It was the first thing she'd said that he could understand.

"I'm a computer programmer. Your grandfather made me apply for this job."

"What?" *His grandfather?* Her obsession with his grandfather had gone totally out of control.

"Of course, I only agreed to apply. I never dreamed you'd hire me. It was his idea to lie about my qualifications, but he had good reason." She slid back the chair and stood, her eyes beseeching. "He wants to meet you, Clayton. He's a wonderful man.

He didn't know your mother was pregnant. He had a nervous breakdown after Martha died. He was sick, devastated from losing everyone he loved. He didn't remember anything until two years later in a hospital in California. Even then he didn't remember who he was or where he was from for another year. That's why he uses the name *Taylor*."

"What?" It was all Clayton could manage to say. Hannah was babbling nonsense.

"That's the name he used to set up his company, so he just kept using it. He didn't see any reason to change back to Sinclair since he didn't know about you until he retired a few months ago, moved back to San Antonio and checked on the ranch to see what had happened to it. He has plenty of money, and he wanted to help you when I told him you were having financial problems, but now you're not."

"I'm not what?"

"Having financial problems. I just explained it to you."

Clayton pinched the bridge of his nose between two fingers and rubbed. He'd heard somewhere that it was supposed to increase blood flow to the brain, clear up the thought processes, and he needed all the mental resources he could find right now.

"Let me get this straight. You've fixed my financial problems, and you have somebody claiming to be my grandfather stashed away somewhere in San Antonio. Is that what you're saying?"

She sighed, looked disgusted and crossed her arms over her breasts. "You don't believe anything I've said, do you?"

"Well, I—"

"I didn't fix your financial problems. You did. The

money was there all along. Your records were just wrong. And the man who lives across the hall from me in San Antonio really is your grandfather. He wants to make it up to you for leaving even though it wasn't his fault.''

Clayton pulled the desk chair over and fell into it. He wasn't sure his legs would support him much longer. It was barely possible Hannah could be telling the truth about his finances. He'd never been much at keeping books.

Was it also possible she was telling the truth about his grandfather, that the man was alive? "How do you know it's really him?''

She looked at the picture over the desk. "It's him.''

Clayton stared at the picture. For all his life his grandfather's memory had been a motivating force in shaping his life. If Hannah was telling the truth, it was more like losing his grandfather than finding him.

"He sent you out here to impersonate a housekeeper and talk me into meeting him?''

"I tried to tell him it would never work. I'm not very good at housekeeping stuff. But I had to try to help him.''

"Because your grandfather died.''

She nodded. "Two months before I received my doctorate, before I could show him his faith in me was justified.''

"You have a doctorate degree?''

Indignant anger stirred Hannah's blood at Clayton's incredulous tone. Maybe her family hadn't been thrilled and proud when she got her degree, but nobody had ever doubted that she did it.

"With honors, as a matter of fact. I told you, I do computers.''

"Yeah, well, you also told me you do housework."

"I did not. As I said, that was all Samuel's idea. I only agreed to come out here because I knew I wouldn't get the job, but then he called your banker and told him that outrageous lie about me working for him."

"Oh, *he* told the lie! So why didn't you tell me the truth? Why did you pretend to be a housekeeper? Why didn't you leave when you saw you couldn't do the job?"

Those were good questions, and Hannah wasn't sure she wanted to face the answers right now. "Because I wanted to help Samuel." That was part of the truth. She didn't need to mention how much she'd wanted to please him, how hard it had been—and still was—to think of leaving and never seeing him again. "Why didn't you fire me when you saw I couldn't do the job?"

He gazed at her for a long moment, his expression changing from accusatory to something she couldn't read. "I don't know," he said quietly. "I meant to. I should have."

The words twisted their way into her heart like a million tiny knives. Serrated knives. He wanted to get rid of her. Nothing that had happened between them—their talks, their touches, not even their kisses—had meant anything to him. It always came back to the same old thing.

In spite of knowing she shouldn't let it get to her, it hurt for someone to judge her and find her lacking because she couldn't accomplish the tasks that person considered important. A person she cared about.

That's where the real problem came in. Somehow she'd let him slip past her defenses. Somehow, she realized with a horrible sinking feeling, she'd let herself fall in love with a man who considered her an inept, bungling, ineffectual housekeeper and didn't think anything else about her could cancel out that failing.

She lifted her chin defiantly. "You don't need to concern yourself about getting rid of me. My purpose in coming here was to tell you about Samuel, and I've done that. Perhaps not as competently as I should have, but to the best of my ability. Now I'm leaving. Your neighbor, Lydia, called today. She's letting her housekeeper go, so you can hire Marjorie and have decent meals and a clean house and clothes with no holes in them."

Proud of herself for her fearless delivery of the facts, she lifted her head high, turned away from Clayton and started out the door. And slammed her shoulder painfully against the jamb. What a time to be clumsy!

"Are you all right?" Clayton was beside her immediately, his hands holding and steadying her.

She pulled away, forcing back the eager hope that flashed over her at his touch. "I'm fine."

"Hannah, don't go like this."

He hadn't said *don't go,* just *don't go like this.* "You don't even like the way I leave? That makes it a hundred percent then. You don't like the way I do anything."

"Yes, I do," he said softly, his gaze holding hers. The room around them blurred, and, as if they were alone in the universe, she could see only Clayton's face. Later she'd consider the intriguing phenomenon, but for the moment, all she could do was swim through this alternate reality.

"What?" she managed to ask. "What do you like?"

He took her arm again, his touch gentle, and for a minute she thought he was going to say something wonderful, something that would change her life forever. But then his eyes hardened. He released her and looked away, breaking the spell, returning them to the quite ordinary room.

"You do lots of things right, Hannah. It's not your fault that you had a few problems out here. This is a harsh place to live, a tough life."

"Oh, good grief! I'm really tired of hearing how tough this place is and how only the strong survive. There's all kinds of tough. You may have lots of muscles on your body but you don't have any in your heart. You call your grandfather weak because he couldn't bear the loss of the people he loved, but at least he had the courage to love. You're afraid to love anything but this ranch because it's the only thing that won't die or leave you, but it can't love you back. You're not so tough after all."

Hannah covered her mouth with her hand. Had she really said those things? She stood in shock, staring at Clayton.

He stared back, apparently in shock, also.

She'd better take the opportunity to get away.

This time, she made it through the doorway without running into either side.

She darted into her room, hurriedly threw her clothes into her suitcase and slammed the lid. The sleeve of a blouse, the hem of a skirt and other bits of clothing stuck out here and there, but she didn't care. They'd make the journey just the same as the parts of the clothes inside the bag.

She threw the two worthless books into the other suitcase, grabbed up both bags and stepped into the hallway. She wouldn't look back toward Clayton, she promised herself. She didn't want to see if he was watching her...if he looked sad to see her go or if he just looked tough. Or worse...if he wasn't even watching.

She heard his footsteps behind her.

"Hannah," he said, "let me carry your bags."

She turned to face him. "No."

She was back to words of one syllable with him. She'd used her quota of words. There was nothing more she wanted to say. All she wanted was for him to take her into his arms and hold her against his solid body and kiss her until she forgot all the hurt surrounding them.

But even if he did, the kiss wouldn't last forever. Eventually they'd have to look around and all the problems would still be there. She'd still be incapable of doing things to make Clayton happy.

She turned and stumbled away as fast as she could go with her suitcases, down the stairs and out the door into the harsh country Clayton professed to love but seemed always to be fighting.

He was missing so much in life, but she couldn't do anything about it. She didn't regret one moment of her love for her grandfather or even her misplaced love for Clayton, though both ended in pain. She wouldn't give back one second of her relationship with Clayton—the wonder of touching him, kissing him, their intimate moments.

But neither would she continue to subject herself to his criticism. Even if he'd wanted her to. Which he didn't. He'd made no effort to follow her down-stairs.

She threw her bags in the back seat of her car, climbed into the front, started the engine and drove away.

Maybe she'd have an empty spot inside for the rest of her life, but she could handle it. In spite of what Clayton thought, she was tough.

From the window of his office, Clayton watched the cloud of dust following Hannah's car as she left.

When Hannah finally figured out how to talk, she sure had a lot to say.

He tried to digest everything she'd told him—his grandfather was alive, the ranch was in the black—but it all skittered across the surface of his mind without sinking in. Only the last scene stuck and pulled him back no matter what he tried to focus on.

Over and over in his head he watched Hannah come from her room with her suitcase sprouting clothing on all sides. Over and over he watched her car pull away and disappear into the dust. He felt as if his heart were inside that dust cloud, bouncing over the sharp rocks and spiny cacti.

Eventually that dust would settle and there would be nothing left to show Hannah had ever been there.

She'd left just as she'd come. Softly and unobtrusively.

But somehow she'd managed to leave a loud, screaming hole in his heart.

He'd thought about trying to stop her.

Except it wouldn't have mattered. So she wasn't an incompetent housekeeper but actually a computer programmer with a doctorate degree. That didn't change anything. She'd never fit in here. She wanted to go back to her comfortable, easy life in the city, and he had no right to stop her. Not even if watching her leave was the hardest thing he'd ever done.

She was right; he'd always made a big deal of how difficult it was to survive out here. Well, he didn't think he'd be saying that again. Not after this experience. Now he knew the real meaning of *tough*.

Thunder boomed loudly and the first drops of rain splatted against the window. Relief from the drought.

If Hannah had been telling the truth—and somehow, he thought she was—his financial difficulties were over. He'd managed to save the ranch.

The rain was a bonus.

And the grandfather he'd wanted to meet so many years ago had returned from the dead...too late, of course.

The long-awaited events failed to bring the happiness he'd expected.

Hannah had walked out the door, yanking his heart right out of his chest.

Chapter Thirteen

Clayton slid back his chair from the table. "Great breakfast, Marjorie."

"It sure was, ma'am," Dub said, and the other men echoed the sentiments.

Hannah had been gone for two weeks. When Dub and the other cowboys had found out she'd left, they'd been upset. But now things were pretty much back to normal.

Pretty much, except Clayton couldn't seem to stop thinking about her. He compared Marjorie's meals to Hannah's, and, of course, Marjorie's won hands down, but he still missed Hannah. Every time he wore a pair of blue jeans or a shirt without holes, he thought about her. Every time he rode back to the house and didn't see her standing on the porch, he thought about her. Every time the sun rose and every time it set, every time he took a breath, he thought about her.

He'd taken her printouts of his financial affairs to

his banker, and Glen had verified that she was right. His banker had even complimented him on his accountant's skills.

Marjorie had taken a call from Samuel Sinclair a couple of days after Hannah left, but Clayton had never returned the call. He had no idea what to say to the man. Even with all Hannah had told him, he still resented the fact that the ranch had meant so little to his grandfather that he hadn't bothered to come back when he'd regained his memory.

Clayton set his hat on his head and opened the front door.

"Uh, Boss, do you mind if we take a few extra minutes this morning before we get back to work?" Dub asked.

Clayton turned to see all the men standing close together, looking a little uncomfortable.

"No, I don't mind. What is it you need to do?"

"Hannah's on the television," Bear announced, a huge grin splitting his beard.

"That early morning talk show out of San Antonio," Bob added.

"Hannah? On television? But she's so shy."

"She said coming out here and doing something she knew she couldn't do made her realize she could go around and talk about her computer games," Dub explained. "Said it taught her that just because you're scared to do something don't mean you can't do it."

"When did she say all this?"

Dub turned his hat in his hands and looked down at his boots. "Uh, well, I...we...talk to her sometimes. On the phone."

"We miss her," Cruiser said. "Just 'cause you all

couldn't get along dudn't mean she's not still our friend.''

"No, of course it doesn't." But he felt betrayed.

They'd been talking to Hannah behind his back.

She'd been talking to them.

He wasn't sure just which side he thought had done the betraying.

Marjorie stepped over and turned on the television. Good grief. She was in on it, too.

The seven of them stood silently while a commercial ran, then the talk show hostess came on and then...

Hannah.

She wore a slim, elegant red suit that set off her dark curls and gave color to her cheeks, and she seemed to be looking directly at him, talking directly to him. She still had that shy demeanor, she still blushed easily, and it was obvious from the applause that the audience found her as charming as he did. She'd come a long way from the day she'd stood on his porch and been unable to speak.

As he watched her, he thought about what Dub had said. She was still frightened. That was obvious. But it wasn't stopping her.

That, perhaps, was the ultimate in courage.

Her fragile appearance and soft-spoken demeanor were deceptive. She wasn't an orchid at all, but a cactus blossom—soft and scented and beautiful yet somehow able to withstand the broiling sun.

Watching her, the hole in his heart got bigger and bigger.

Another commercial came on, taking her away from him.

"Hannah done good," Mugger said.

"Sure did," Bob agreed.

Everyone started out of the room, Marjorie back to the kitchen and the cowboys to work.

"Is that all?" Clayton asked. She couldn't be gone so soon. He wanted to see her again, to hear her again.

"Yep, that's all," Bear said. "She sure did look pretty, didn't she?"

"Dub, wait a minute," he called after the departing men.

Dub returned.

"Uh, sit down for a minute." He motioned him to the chair Hannah had sat in a lifetime ago.

"Something wrong?"

"No, nothing. You, uh, mentioned that you'd talked to Hannah. I just wondered what she had to say." He knew it was crazy, but he just had to hear Hannah again, even if it was secondhand.

Dub lifted an ankle over one knee and fiddled with the hem of his blue jeans. "She didn't have a whole lot to say. Hannah never was one to talk your ear off."

"I know that. What did she say?" *Did she ask about me?*

"Well, let me see. She finished another game. *Unicorn in the Garden.* Mostly she talked about this tour and how excited she was and how scared she was."

"Did she ask about, uh, the ranch?"

"Yes, she did. And I told her how much the rains have helped and how good everything's going. Told her Marjorie's working out fine."

Clayton's jaw clenched in frustration. He wanted to grab Dub by the shoulders and shake him. Dub wasn't dumb. He never missed a thing. He knew what

Clayton wanted to know. Was the man going to make him ask the question?

"Guess you wish you hadn't let her leave," Dub said suddenly.

"I had no choice. I told you that already." But he'd just admitted to himself that she wasn't the hothouse flower he'd believed her to be. Had he been too hasty in his judgment? "Anyway, what makes you think she would have stayed if I'd asked her to?"

"'Course she would have. That girl's plumb crazy about you. Anybody could see that."

Clayton's chest lit inside like a summer sunrise. "Why do you say that?" he asked, trying to sound unconcerned. "Not that it matters."

Dub shook his head. "'Course it matters. If it didn't, you wouldn't have been going around here the last couple of weeks looking like you lost your best friend. You'd be happier'n a rabbit in a clover patch what with the mortgage paid off and the rains breaking the drought and cattle prices going up."

"I *am* happy about all that."

Dub rose from the chair and shook his head again. "No, you're not. I reckon you're in the same boat your granddaddy was in."

No wonder he'd stood up. He was getting ready to run for his life after making a comment like that.

"You've lost your mind. I have nothing in common with my grandfather."

"Sure you do. You love that woman so much, the ranch just don't matter anymore."

Clayton shot off the sofa. "That's ridiculous." He stood eyeball to eyeball with Dub, but Dub refused to back down.

"All this business about letting Hannah leave because you know she's not tough enough to make it out here is just hogwash,'' he said, his voice as calm and matter-of-fact as if they'd been discussing which cows were due to calve. ''Hannah can do anything she wants to do. You saw that a few minutes ago on the television. No, what you're worried about is yourself. Samuel lost Martha. Your mom lost your dad. Sure as shooting, if you love somebody, somewhere along the way, it's gonna hurt. But it's pretty dumb to bring that pain on yourself before you have all the good years you can first. Seems like your granddad knew that and you don't.''

Dub shoved his hat onto his head and walked away leaving Clayton gazing after him in shock.

Dub had said, in a different way, the same things Hannah had said before she'd left.

Which meant they were both wrong.

He pushed out the door. He needed to get to work and forget all this nonsense.

Like you've forgotten Hannah? that annoying little voice asked. If that voice had a body, he'd kick it in the rear.

As he stepped outside, Dub, standing on the edge of the porch, turned and lifted a silencing finger to his lips then pointed into the yard.

The porcupine was not only still around, but now there were two.

''The porcupine takes a wife,'' Dub whispered.

''How do you know that's a female?''

''Look at them. They're obviously in love.''

''They are? How can you tell? How can they even get close to each other with those quills?''

''Love will find a way. Guess you were wrong about that little fellow. I don't think he has any intention of leaving. Before you know it, we'll have a whole herd of porcupines around here."

Clayton watched the two creatures lumbering along together. They seemed blissfully happy, unaware of the problems facing them.

Clayton realized he was envious.

"Here's to bigger and bigger successes." Samuel handed Hannah a glass of cola, touched his own glass to hers, then sat down in his recliner.

"Thanks." Hannah leaned back on Samuel's comfortable, textured beige sofa and sipped her soda.

"You were fantastic on that television show," Samuel continued. "I'm really proud of you. And I know your own grandfather is, too. He was right, you know. You can do anything you want to do."

Not quite anything, she thought. She hadn't been able to make Clayton love her.

"I guess one good thing came of my going out to the ranch. After cooking all those meals for your grandson and the cowboys when I had no idea what I was doing, anything else pales in comparison. I did something I have no aptitude for, I did it badly and yet Dub and the other guys like me. They still want to be friends." She smiled. "You could say I learned that failure won't kill me."

"Very true," he agreed. "The only failure that will kill you is failure to get up and try again."

"It still bothers me, though, that I wasn't able to get Clayton to talk to you. I know you wanted that very badly. He hasn't called you back, has he?"

Samuel shook his head, a sad half-smile playing about his lips. "Don't let that bother you. As soon as spring roundup is over, I'm planning to drive out to the ranch and confront my grandson. Then we'll see what happens.'' His smile widened to a grin. "I think I'd better confess something so you can stop worrying that you let me down. My primary goal in sending you out there wasn't to smooth the way for me. I'm afraid I told a little white lie.''

Hannah sat upright on the sofa. "Another one? You mean one besides making Clayton's banker give me a reference?''

Samuel waved a negligent hand. "Oh, this one's much bigger than that one. You see, about the time you and I became friends, I'd just gotten back the reports from my detective about my grandson. I realized from what the neighbors said about him and from his life-style that he was a very lonely man.''

Hannah nodded agreement. "He's afraid to love anything but that ranch.''

"I know. And I felt somewhat responsible for his problem. If I'd been around, he'd have had an easier life and things would have probably been different. So, looking around me, I noticed that my dear friend, Hannah, was also lonely.''

"I was not!''

"This is my story,'' he reprimanded gently. "Anyway, I decided if my grandson met my dear friend, Hannah, perhaps neither one of them would be lonely any longer, and I'd have a grandson and a granddaughter and I wouldn't be lonely any longer either.''

Hannah blinked twice, trying to take in what Samuel was saying. "You were matchmaking?'' she finally managed to whisper.

"I'm afraid I was. So you see, I'm the one who failed in this endeavor, not you. But you did admit you got something out of the experience, which means it wasn't a total failure.''

Hannah stared at him in stunned disbelief. ''You conned me! You manipulated me!''

''Guilty. But I had good intentions.''

He'd hoped she and Clayton would get together, would fall in love.

He'd never know how close he'd come to succeeding, at least on her part.

She tried to work up some anger at Samuel's actions, but couldn't find any. She'd have been as thrilled as he to be his granddaughter, to wake up every morning next to Clayton and go to sleep every night in his arms.

''It didn't work,'' she said, assuring herself that the little ache somewhere in the vicinity of her heart was only indigestion caused by topping off her peanut butter and blackberry jam sandwich with a frozen burrito at lunch.

He shrugged. ''I'm sorry it didn't, but if the chemistry's not there, nobody can create it.''

Involuntarily, Hannah recalled the way Clayton's lips had molded to hers, the power of his heart pounding wildly against her breast...

Oh, the chemistry had been there!

But so had reality. She'd been found wanting in the skills that mattered to Clayton.

She couldn't judge him for that, for being who he was. He was no more able to change that than she could change herself.

Just as her parents had been unable to change their ideas of what they needed from her. They'd been thrilled with her upcoming publicity tour and television appearance that morning on a local station. But

Hannah had been surprised to find that pleasing them no longer mattered to her. She was glad they were happy, but she'd been prepared to deal with their displeasure.

She'd never fit their mold, any more than she could fit Clayton's. She had her own mold into which she fit very nicely, and she was no longer going to apologize to anyone for it or try to change into someone she wasn't and didn't even want to be.

A distant rumble of thunder interrupted her thoughts. "I'd better get home," she said. "I left my windows open, and it looks like rain."

"Sure does. That's good. The old homestead can use a little more."

Samuel gazed out the window with a faintly wistful expression, one less dramatic but, she suspected, more genuine than when he'd been manipulating her into going out to the ranch.

She could accept that Clayton and she would never be together, but blast the man for refusing to at least talk to his own grandfather!

She went to where Samuel sat, leaned over and gave him a hug. "See you later."

He patted her shoulder and smiled. "You can count on it."

Hannah stepped into the hall.

And saw Clayton leaning against the door of her unit.

She whirled around just in time to see Samuel give her a *thumbs-up* sign and quietly close the door behind her.

Clayton pushed his hat back off his forehead. "Hi," he said, his voice and expression just a little uncertain, she thought.

"How'd you get past the security door downstairs?"

"I carried in some lady's groceries. Everybody trusts a cowboy."

Not everybody, she thought. *Not me.*

"What are you doing here? Is this more of Samuel's doing?"

He looked a little sheepish but genuinely puzzled. "I haven't talked to Samuel."

"Why not? I know he tried to call you."

A neighbor walked out into the hall and eyed them curiously before heading...very slowly...toward the elevator.

"Could we go inside to discuss this?" Clayton asked.

Hannah hesitated, biting her lip. In spite of fantasies that sometimes burst unexpectedly into the midst of her computer work, she knew they had nothing to discuss.

Not to mention that, as bent out of shape as he got about her housekeeping problems on the ranch, he'd flip when he saw the disorder of her home.

"Okay," he said when she made no move to open her door. "We can do this out here." He swept off his hat and fell to one knee in front of her. "Hannah Lindsay, I—"

Hannah leapt closer to him, spreading her skirt as if she could hide him from prying eyes. "Are you crazy?"

The elevator stopped, but the neighbor let it go without her and stood unabashedly watching the show.

Hurriedly Hannah unlocked her door and darted inside. Clayton followed.

"No empty chairs," she warned, waving a hand around the room. "Sit on the floor or move something." She settled in her desk chair and looked at him, waiting nervously for him to finish what he'd started to say in the hallway. Normally when a man knelt before a woman—

As if anything in her relationship with Clayton was normal.

There she went with the fantasies again.

He moved a couple of books to the floor and sat on the sofa. "I saw you on television this morning. You were terrific."

"Thank you." Clayton's words, his voice, the look in his eyes, all washed over her like liquid sunshine. She wanted him to go on, to allow her to bask in the glow forever, but it was pointless. Just because she'd done a television show didn't mean anything had changed between Clayton and her.

Besides, she had a responsibility, an unfinished obligation. Even if Samuel had denied his purpose in sending her to the ranch, she knew he desperately wanted a reunion with Clayton. And Clayton needed a grandfather. "Why haven't you returned Samuel's phone call?"

He ran distracted fingers through his hair. "I don't know. I've been busy."

She lifted an eyebrow.

"Okay, I haven't been *that* busy. I just—" He shrugged. "I wasn't sure what to say."

"Clayton—"

He lifted a hand to forestall her protest. "I know. I understand now why he acted the way he did." He shifted uneasily, leaning forward with his elbows on his knees, turning his hat in his hands. Could confident Clayton be nervous?

"You were right," he said, studying his hat intently. "It seemed like everybody I loved or could have loved left the ranch, left me. I wasn't tough enough to risk that happening again. I wasn't tough enough to love." He raised his eyes to her. "Until you, Hannah. You kind of slipped in on my blind side."

"I did?" Clayton couldn't possibly mean what it sounded like he meant.

A slow grin spread over his face. "Well, actually, it was more like you stumbled in."

She lifted her chin defiantly. "Maybe I'm not always graceful and maybe I can't do everything you can, but you can't do everything I can, either."

"I know. We kind of complement each other, don't we? It takes the two of us to make a whole." He rose and, taking care to step over the books and computer disks littering the floor, walked over to her.

He took her hands and urged her up then pulled her into his arms. It was a place she'd thought she'd never be again.

Without conscious thought, she slid her arms around him, and couldn't stop herself from luxuriating in the glorious feel of his solid body pressing against her.

"Hannah, I'm having a hard time with words right now, but I'm trying to tell you that I love you."

"You do?" Suddenly her vocal chords pulled their old trick of tightening up on her, making her words come out squeaky.

"I do. Thanks to your expertise in correcting my bad bookkeeping, I don't have to worry about paying off the mortgage on the ranch. We've had enough rain over the past couple of weeks to end the drought. Cattle prices are up. Everything about the ranch is wonderful." He pushed her hair back from her face and trailed a finger down her cheek. "Everything but my heart. Everything but having the woman I love beside me. And without her, none of the rest seems very important."

Had she heard right? The ranch wasn't important?

"Hannah, can you give me a clue where I stand? I'm not tough enough to throw my heart out to you and not know if you feel the same. Is there any chance you could love a cowboy? This cowboy?"

Amazing. Clayton was capable of being every bit as insecure as she was.

Her throat muscles relaxed. She gave a short, giddy laugh. "Yes. Of course I do. I do love you."

It wasn't an eloquent answer, but it must have been the right one. He lowered his lips to hers, and she knew what he meant about only being complete when they were together. With his kiss, he seemed to share all of himself, his ability to dance, to talk…heck, she could probably ride a horse and herd cattle now. For sure, he took her on a dragon ride to the stars.

He pulled away, just far enough to look into her eyes. "I know the ranch is out in the middle of nowhere and it's dusty and dirty and there's no soft green grass and the house is old and dark and you'd probably want to redecorate." His gaze slid sideways to scan her living room. "Or maybe you wouldn't. Maybe we could get a professional decorator. What I'm trying to say is, if you'll marry me, I'll do whatever it takes to make you comfortable out there."

A slow smile stretched up from her chest all the

way to her lips. "Marry you. Go to sleep in your arms every night and wake up there every morning."

"At five o'clock every morning."

She flinched. "I guess I agree to the early morning thing if you promise never to try to keep your books or even touch the computer again."

"*Our* books. I promise. If you promise you'll never cook, clean house or do the laundry."

"Deal!" *Thank goodness!*

He lowered his mouth to hers again. Just before she gave up conscious thought in favor of exquisite sensations, Hannah noticed that her nose went to exactly the right spot. A good sign.

Several minutes and kisses later, Hannah pushed away from his arms and took his hand. "Come with me," she said. "There's someone I want you to meet."

Epilogue

The organist struck up "The Wedding March." At the back of the century-old Spanish church, Hannah took her father's arm, sucked in a deep breath and started down the aisle, praying she wouldn't fall off the two-inch heels her mother had insisted were appropriate instead of flats. At least her gown was ankle-length, so she didn't have to worry about tripping on it.

Samuel had located Martha's wedding dress, stored safely away in a box in the attic, and Hannah felt honored and cherished to be wearing it. The simple, classic lines of the ivory satin were timeless, and the fit was perfect, except that Hannah was taller than Martha had been, making the dress shorter. Thank goodness.

She lifted her gaze to the front of the church, to Clayton and to Samuel standing beside him, his best man in all senses of the word.

From the moment she had led Clayton through the

door of Samuel's condo, the two men had bonded as if they'd been together all their lives. Though Samuel spent a lot of time at his old home and had been able to pass on invaluable information and assistance on the ranch, he still refused to move back into the house.

She and Clayton had finally persuaded him, however, to have a small house built on the land, within walking distance of the ranch house. He'd agreed so his great-grandchildren could come over every day.

As she approached, Clayton gave her a smile and a wink. He was undoubtedly as uncomfortable in the tuxedo as she was in the heels, but he didn't look uncomfortable. He looked glorious, even without his hat. His eyes were bright and full of love, and she knew if she kept her gaze locked on him, she wouldn't stumble.

"Your mother and I are so proud of you, baby," her father whispered as they reached the front.

She wasn't sure why her father made the comment—because she'd come out of her shell or because she hadn't tripped going down the aisle. And it didn't matter.

She was proud of herself for being the best she could be. Clayton was proud enough of her to make her his bride, the future mother of his children. Those were the things that mattered.

"Who gives this woman in marriage?"

"Her mother and I."

Hannah's father put her hand into Clayton's. Her soon-to-be husband beamed down at her, and she knew that the ritual passing was very real. She was going from a time of feeling insecure and unloved to a lifetime of love.

Heck, she might even be able to learn to dance.

Her feet in the unaccustomed heels tangled as she turned to face the minister and only Clayton's strong arm saved her from falling.

She'd probably better forget the dancing and settle for undying love and sole access to the computer.

*   *   *   *   *

Silhouette Romance proudly invites you
to get to know the members of

The Single Daddy Club

a new miniseries by award-winning author
Donna Clayton

Derrick: Ex-millitary man who unexpectedly
falls into fatherhood
MISS MAXWELL BECOMES A MOM (March '97)

Jason: Widowed daddy desperately in need of some live-in help
NANNY IN THE NICK OF TIME (April '97)

Reece: Single and satisfied father of one about
to meet his Ms. Right
BEAUTY AND THE BACHELOR DAD (May '97)

Don't miss any of these heartwarming stories as
three single dads say bye-bye to their bachelor days.
Only from

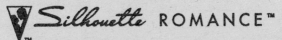

Silhouette ROMANCE™

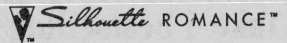
Silhouette ROMANCE™

cordially invites you to the unplanned nuptials
of three unsuspecting hunks and their

SURPRISE BRIDES

Look for the following specially packaged titles:

March 1997: MISSING: ONE BRIDE by Alice Sharpe, #1212
April 1997: LOOK-ALIKE BRIDE by Laura Anthony, #1220
May 1997: THE SECRET GROOM by Myrna Mackenzie, #1225

Don't miss **Surprise Brides**, an irresistible trio of books about love
and marriage by three talented authors! Found only in—

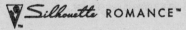
Silhouette ROMANCE™

As seen on TV!
Free Gift Offer

With a Free Gift proof-of-purchase from any Silhouette® book,
you can receive a beautiful cubic zirconia pendant.

This gorgeous marquise-shaped stone is a genuine cubic
zirconia—accented by an 18" gold tone necklace.

(Approximate retail value $19.95)

Send for yours today...

compliments of *Silhouette*®

To receive your free gift, a cubic zirconia pendant, send us one original proof-of-
purchase, photocopies not accepted, from the back of any Silhouette Romance™,
Silhouette Desire®, Silhouette Special Edition®, Silhouette Intimate Moments®
or Silhouette Yours Truly™ title available in February, March and April at your favorite
retail outlet, together with the Free Gift Certificate, plus a check or money order for
$1.65 U.S./$2.15 CAN. (do not send cash) to cover postage and handling, payable
to Silhouette Free Gift Offer. We will send you the specified gift. Allow 6 to 8 weeks for
delivery. Offer good until April 30, 1997 or while quantities last. Offer valid in the
U.S. and Canada only.

Free Gift Certificate

Name: _____

Address: _____

City: _____ State/Province: _____ Zip/Postal Code: _____

Mail this certificate, one proof-of-purchase and a check or money order for postage
and handling to: SILHOUETTE FREE GIFT OFFER 1997. In the U.S.: 3010 Walden
Avenue, P.O. Box 9077, Buffalo NY 14269-9077. In Canada: P.O. Box 613, Fort Erie,
Ontario L2Z 5X3.

FREE GIFT OFFER   084-KFD

ONE PROOF-OF-PURCHASE
To collect your fabulous FREE GIFT, a cubic zirconia pendant, you must include this
original proof-of-purchase for each gift with the properly completed Free Gift Certificate.

084-KFD

In April 1997
Bestselling Author

DALLAS SCHULZE

takes her Family Circle series to new heights with

TESSA'S CHILD

In April 1997 Dallas Schulze brings readers a
brand-new, longer, out-of-series title featuring the
characters from her popular Family Circle miniseries.

When rancher Keefe Walker found Tessa Wyndham he
knew that she needed a man's protection—she was
pregnant, alone and on the run from a heartless past.
Keefe was also hiding from a dark past...but in one
overwhelming moment he and Tessa forged a family
bond that could never be broken.

Available in April wherever books are sold.